Whispers of Summer

Violet Langley

CONTENTS

CHAPTER 1

Willow sat by the window, playing with the curtain's tassel and looking wistfully outside at the two strolling figures. Her dark hair hung loosely about her neck, the curls from yesterday had unwound and instead of being their usual glossy ebony colour, they seemed faded. In her free hand, she was holding her woven country hat, rather carelessly and with a loose grip. She had been watching the couple for ten minutes now as they walked up and down the nearby fields. The stout mother, who had been watching Willow since she entered the sitting room, would frequently put her knitting work down, open her mouth as if to speak, then pick up her knitting again and continue in silence. Another ten minutes passed in this fashion, whilst Willow continued to hit the tassel harder and at more frequent intervals. At length, the mother put her knitting down again and thus decided it was time to speak.

"Now, who is it you are watching, dear? Is it Kitty?" Of course, she knew most definitely it was Kitty; who else would Willow be so looking so wistfully at?

The girl turned her head to face her mother and her deflated dark mop of hair turned with her. "Sadly, yes, dear mama, and she is with Lord Rosewood's son; he's just come from the city, you see mama, since his father's been feeling so ill lately."

"I am sure Lord Rosewood will feel better soon enough, he is prone to getting ill so easily, even in this warmer weather."

Willow sighed an exasperated sigh. "I wonder why he never came before if his father is ill often. I'm afraid it must be a little more severe this time."

There was a silence as her mother figured out what to say next for she was never good with words. "Hopefully he will be alright."

Willow turned back to the window and her dark eyes glistened with a mingled sense of jealousy and admiration. "Kitty's awfully lucky, mother. Look at her, getting all of the attention from him-him!" She felt the need to repeat that word. "The most eligible gentleman that will come to visit the country this whole year and possibly the next.

"You mustn't blame Kitty for it though. I'm sure she can't help it--"

"Yes, of course, she can't help it; she's too busy being the wonderful girl that she is. How am I supposed to compare to that? I'll never win when she's there. Why must she be the same age as me? I don't understand how it can be fair at all. Mama," she lifted her head up with a few traces of hope, "when will we all be introduced to Mr Rosewood?"

"At the party the Richards will host, I suppose." She paused, looking about her as though the words should appear behind some furniture in the room. "Then, you'd be grateful of Kitty, wouldn't you?"

Willow felt that a reply wasn't needed. Instead, she stood up and placed her hat on her head with a rough hand and tapped it firmly, giving the impression that she was gluing it to her head. "I think I ought to go for a walk, mama."

"What, join them?" The mother seemed happy at this change in mood.

"No, on my own. Although I wish Charlie would come back from the town, I'm feeling so friendless without him. It's a shame he isn't here to talk about Kitty with me."

"It should teach you a lesson, child. You two are always saying things about the poor girl-"

"Why, it isn't half as bad as you think," Willow began with an earnest tone, "he's quite fond of her himself. I wouldn't blame him though; it's past him, for she's a lot cleverer than he thinks her to be."

Her mother said with a knotted eyebrows, "I hope you'd convince him to be more civil to her then, rather than persuade him to think of her as you do."

"Me remind him to be civil to her?" She laughed then checked herself. "Anyway, I'm off now. I'll be back soon, before it's dark."

Willow planted a kiss on her mother's cheek and was about to bolt out of the door, when her mother reminded her, "Do fix your hair, Willow, for if you should meet someone on the way it would be dreadful."

With that, Willow left with her hair fixed as best as she could manage. She went trotting down the familiar laneways, walking past the tall trees and smelling their strong scent along the way. It was a warm February evening, the ground beneath cool enough for her to take off her slippers and walk bare feet for a while. If it was not for the biting ants she would have considered going this way for all of her walk, but the thought of being bitten by those ants all over her feet was not something Willow was fond of. There was no general movement in the area, with the exception of a few late workers returning home and the occasional couple of friends taking an evening stroll before dinner would be served.

She was quite conscious of the fact that she was noting Charlie's absence much more than she anticipated, but it was only two weeks until he would return, so she found herself fortunate in that regard. Usually, the two of them would walk together, exchanging stories about their day, with a joke or two from Charlie's side, and of course, every now and then he'd bring a sweet for her. And now, the realisation that she'd have to walk alone for another two weeks after having endured a single lonesome week, seemed to present itself every day at about this particular time of the day. Sometimes she thought it would have been better if he had left during the winter, but that wish was soon discarded since she positively knew she could not bear cold evenings stuck indoors with no jolly, youthful company.

Her circle of friends was comprised of him and two girls her own age who she was not particular about. Willow thought them too chatty beyond their own good and their hopeless way of copying everything that Kitty did, which made them easy targets for her scorn, absolutely repelled her from advancing the friendship further.

There were plenty of young men that was true, but everyone in the community seemed to be settled and promised already. Kitty being boastful of her family's connection to the English peerage, in some odd, complicated way that Willow never quite understood, thought that she deserved the best of the best, to put it simply. And with the gentleman who sported such another 'connection to the English peerage', married to a lovely, bright lady (who Willow thought to be a hundred times better than Kitty) from the nearby town, Kitty sought for the next best she could find; the simple-hearted, but dangerously wealthy, Charles. Now, was it Willow's job to protect her friend from that superficial lady?

Willow thought so, but there was a limit to what she could do. Warn, she did and, it is very true, that the good Charles listened and believed, but slowly he had been won over. And how did Willow burn with anger then nearly weep with pity for her friend when Mr Rosewood came to visit and Kitty set her sights on him!

Her letters to Charlie upheld a calm, cheerful tone for she thought it would have been cruel to break his heart in such a way. He would realise for himself when he returned and she could only hope he would understand and forget about her. But, Willow knew her friend well, and she was sometimes troubled by the thought that he would instead attempt to challenge Mr Rosewood and let Kitty decide who she wanted best.

Her mind was wondering about such things when she came to a tumultuous thump onto the ground, having bumped with great force into another evening walker who was lost in his thoughts as she was.

The soft and calm, yet manly assertive voice apologised before she had a chance herself, "I'm deeply sorry, miss. Here, let me get that for you." He picked up the straw hat and handed it back to her.

Willow jumped a step back when she looked up to meet the face that smiled at her with tender sorrow and concern. A moment later, trying to compose herself, she took the hat back and placed it on

her head. "Why, Mr Rosewood, I'm glad to make your acquaintance."
Willow didn't need anything further but to see his expensive shoes
to know whom it was. She paused and made a mistake by looking
into his charming brown eyes as his face moved to form a warm
smile. Recollecting herself, she stammered, "I- I mean, I ought to
have apologised first. Very sorry, Mr Rosewood."

"Don't be really; I should have been looking where I was going.
I was thinking and I've got a terrible habit of walking fast when I
do and I knocked you quite clear."

Willow looked down, knowing that it was she who was walking
fast and he was walking slowly and softly, for she didn't hear any
footsteps walking that way.

"You know me, but I fear I haven't had the pleasure of being
introduced to you."

Willow speedily introduced herself and was more than welcome
of shaking his hand cordially. She was thankful for the shining
moon that night, for it illuminated his face so wonderfully and,
rather vainly, she was also sure that it made her hair look more
agreeable than it was.

"Why, you must be a friend of Miss Richards' then?" There came
the dreaded question, but it was delivered with such melodious
tones of voice that Willow could have forgotten all of her dislike
for Kitty.

"Yes, I am. She's quite wonderful, is she not?" Willow had to force
herself to say the last sentence and hoped her struggle couldn't
be noticed in her voice, but indeed, it was.

"I've heard enough to satisfy me from Miss Richards today on
her personal achievements of character. I'd like to hear from you
tonight," he paused to peer at his waistcoat watch briefly and

resumed, "I believe you're returning home by this time. Do you mind me accompanying you?"

"Not at all, Mr Rosewood, I would be delighted." She took the arm that he offered to her and was thanking her lucky stars that she had bumped into him.

CHAPTER 2

They walked on talking of general things; the climate that he had to be accustomed to as of moving to this region, the people who lived here, and the various little shops and places to visit. Willow found him to be absolutely charming, so considerate of her feelings, yet able to throw in a merry jest in here and there. He was far more intellectual than she thought he would be and found that he knew a great deal more than any of the young men from the area. She was delighted to find that he was definitely handsome because she did know of people who only look pleasant when you first meet them or when viewed from particular angle. He was endowed with stunning dark brown eyes that were warm and open; they had a habit of hovering around her when she spoke that Willow had to stop herself from blushing.

The young gentleman had a lively complexion; he wasn't lacking in colour and had an overall warm brown tone. Willow thought that he had taken quite a liking to her character because he began to ask questions about what she thought of certain authors, artists and composers. She answered all of the questions earnestly, hoping that her simple tastes would not send him away. However, they seemed to do quite the opposite, for, somewhere in the middle of their conversation he made a statement.

"You are quite a refreshing young lady to speak to. I must say, your tastes in the modern are so rare amongst other people our age. For some reason they think it to be the trait of a superior character to pretend to have interests in art they have never had the pleasure of seeing, music they have never heard or played, and even literature they have never read. I can associate with just about everything that you have named. You seem to be the best of the lot around here." He said that last sentence with a hint of mischief that seemed to be naturally followed by a small wink.

"Well, I wouldn't be so quick, Mr Rosewood, for you would find many other people here—both ladies and gentlemen—to be of the same opinion as you and I. It isn't something so uncommon—"

"I find that hard to believe, Miss—"

She couldn't help but interrupt, "You may call me Willow, Mr Rosewood."

Pleased, his face moved slowly into that warm smile of his once again and Willow was certain that he had brought her arm closer to him with a much firmer grasp as well. "Thank you, and feel free to call me Arthur if you wish." He paused for a while and looked at her with a pleased smile, "You know, I think I'd like to know you better. What will you be doing tomorrow after breakfast?"

Realising that they had reached the bottom of the hill where her house was situated, Willow knew that this question was a proposal to meet again another time. "I'll be at the market to buy a few things, but, if you wouldn't mind the simple shops that we have,

I'd be happy to have you with me." The last words came without thought and they made her blush slightly.

"You'll see me there," was the short reply that he gave, but that was all that was needed to make Willow even more reluctant to leave his side.

"Why, I guess I should go now, Mr Rosewood. Thank you very much for accompanying me and I'm awfully sorry for bumping you."

"No need to apologise, dear," the way he said that word made Willow's feet feel like they were glued to the ground—why must she leave, could the night not wait a while! "I must bid you adieu now, but we'll meet again tomorrow."

"Goodnight, Mr Rosewood. Thanks again," and this time she walked briskly up to her house, looking back once or twice along the way. And when she reached the door, she stood there for a while, watching him walk off, hands in pockets and whistling a merry tune.

CHAPTER 3

Over dinner, Willow related the meeting to her mother, saving a few details for her to continue to think about the next morning. Her mother was definitely happy that her daughter's mood had been restored, but expressed her worries of her coming home late even on summer nights. The next day, she spent extra time dressing, making sure that every particular was agreeable; not too plain, but she still didn't want to make it seem as though she had placed extra effort on her dress.

As she checked her face in the looking glass she hoped that Charles wouldn't continue giving her so many chocolates all of the time. Breakfast had been eaten quickly and the morning duties rushed, for she could not bear the thought of keeping Mr Rosewood waiting.

Whilst walking to the market, Willow tried keeping a steady pace, but she ended up half-running the whole way, with one hand holding onto her basket and the other fixing her hair. Finally, she reached the market; it was essentially a main road with the two sides filled with shops of every useful variety—a butcher, a florist, a greengrocer, a hairdresser, a shoe shop, et cetera. Willow pushed on through the crowd, trying to find Mr Rosewood or find a spot where she was sure he would be able to see her if he arrived later. However, she did not have to walk very far before she reached the only bookshop in the small town and saw the gentleman standing there, clutching a tattered volume in his hands.

She stood where she was, a little away from him, watching with admiration. His hat was removed and placed on the bench of books in front of him; the deep brown curly locks on his head covered his forehead as he tilted his head forwards into the tiny book. He seemed so much at peace there, amongst the second-hand volumes of old classics; his new summer clothes in stark contrasts with everything around him. After two minutes of careful examination, she approached him and brought herself to say 'Good morning' as coolly as she could.

He immediately lowered the book and shook back his locks, "Good morning, my dear—" He faltered as he read her face for a reaction, seeing that he made no offense, he smiled and continued, "How are you?"

"Good, Mr Rosewood. And you?" Was the simple reply.

"Well, very well. I've found this wonderful volume of some country ballads and I had someone in mind to—" That was a deliberate mistake, Willow was sure, "But never mind that. I've got to buy it."

So she accompanied him inside as he made the transaction and they were soon browsing rows of shelves in the bookshop. For years, Willow thought it to be a huge collection, but she was willing to discard that belief as soon as Mr Rosewood began speaking of the 'limited nature of this small, provincial bookstore'. Their conversation on books soon changed to a more general one.

"And who are your usual friends, Willow, besides Miss Richards?"

How I'd like to tell you, she thought, what I really think about that Miss Richards of yours!

She talked of the other young ladies who she was acquainted with.

"But who are you closest with?"

"That would be Mr Daniel, we're such close friends."

He cast those laughing eyes towards her all at once with that same air of mischief that they had the previous evening when he winked. "I knew there would have been a gentleman under all of those names."

"Oh, but we're merely friends—"

"I know," he looked indifferently at the words on the spine of a row of books, "I never said anything about that." Then he moved his gaze back upon her and having quite fulfilled his goal of getting her cheeks to colour he stated as he loosened his necktie. "It's stuffy in here; I came to the country to have some fresh air, so let's get out."

Willingly to get out as soon as possible, she followed him out the door as quickly as he led the way. Once they were out into the street again, he made himself civil by abstaining from asking other questions while she finished her shopping. Then, he resumed his former tone.

"What would you say Mr Daniel is like?"

"Well, he's an agreeable young fellow and quite nice."

"I hoped he would be," he smiled more to himself than to her.

"Why do you say that?"

"Since he's your friend, you see. He'd have to be agreeable and nice and all those other things. May I ask one more question, dear?"

She would have refused him were it not for his use of that amicable tone and that affectionate word. "Sure, but I wish you would stop quizzing me."

"Do you think we could be friends? I mean, I'd like to see us near friends now."

"Wh-why, I couldn't see why not."

That was more than he needed to take the basket from her and offer her his free arm. "There, now I'm quite an agreeable fellow too, aren't I?"

Willow checked herself from permitting him to even think that she was weak-minded. "Yes, that is quite right. But don't you think it is my turn to ask some questions?"

CHAPTER 4

"Go ahead," he threw his head back and his curls jostled about his face.

She asked of his friends and what they were like, and he gave rather general answers. So, instead she asked of his family, "And do you have any siblings?"

"I have an older and a younger sister, you should meet them one day."

She asked of his father's health next, which was met with a reply that she would have never anticipated.

'What, you think that old story's real? For some strange reason, Willow, there have been some stories that the only reason I've come to the country is because my father's ill. He's not one to fall ill, ever, and I'd be very concerned if he was, not half as happy as I am now. You oughtn't to believe that story, it isn't real."

"Then, why have you come to the country? It is your first time since you left, why now?"

He hesitated, "To tell the truth, I needed to sort some things out on the family's estate. Nothing much really and it shouldn't keep me long."

She thought for a few moments and a silence passed between them. "We have recently met Mr Rosewood so forgive my question if it bothers you, but you speak of sorting out some things on the family estate does this mean that there is a certain engagement of sorts?"

He had to think about what she meant and paused a while. Willow realised that he looked as handsome as ever even when his eyebrows were knotted and his face hard at work, thinking. "What, you talk of marriage? No, nothing of the sort." He laughed heartily, although she wished he wouldn't because it seemed as though she was the subject of his ridicule. "Oh, but you mustn't think I'm laughing at you, Willow, only at the thought of me getting married anytime soon."

So, you don't have any intentions in mind with Miss Richards? She felt like asking, but she knew it would be detrimental to this blossoming acquaintanceship, so she let the matter be and dropped the subject altogether.

When they were back onto the familiar fields of the nearby farms, they reached interesting conversation again.

"You know the Richards are to have a party," he began, "something that the lovely (if you don't mind me calling her that) Miss Richards has thought up. Well, if you haven't heard of it—as I think you don't, judging from your reaction just now—you will soon. I'm sure Miss Richards wouldn't exclude you. So, you remember this old book I bought," he brought out the book from his pocket, "well, I remembered just how much Miss Richards says she has been practicing country ballads and how she would wish she had some sort of reliable copy, something old she says, so I think this volume of love ballads will do very well. And don't you think it such a fitting gift; show me a young lady who wouldn't want a book of love ballads as a present?"

He turned to face her and produced one of those earnest smiles, which left Willow no choice but to take that comment less seriously as she thought she should have and with perhaps less doubt of a hidden meaning than she would have otherwise thought. "Miss Richards says she shall sing and play to the company on the night and I hear she's quite the skilled musician, so I think I ought to familiarise myself with some of these myself, for I'm sure she'll call for me to accompany her. You, being so long acquainted with her, have heard her sing?"

Without much enthusiasm, Willow replied, "Yes, I have. You will find Miss Richards to be a fitting companion for singing, that is if her vocal talents do not surpass yours as I highly think they will." There was a tinge of revenge in her voice as she gave him a bitter comment in return for his, but she couldn't execute hers as naturally as he could.

"Why, is that a challenge? I think you underestimate my musical abilities, Willow, and you'll be surprised to know that I've got quite an enchanting voice, if I do say so myself. I can play the pianoforte not as bad as you probably think and I've also gotten a grasp at the banjo, and I doubt you've ever heard such a fine musician as me." Looking at her with a clever, planned smile. "Though think yourself lucky that you won't have to wait very long until you hear me sing. And at that, it'll be a love ballad I'll be singing. . . " He trailed off and purposely left her to ponder the thought with her own imagination.

As soon as Willow was beginning to forget about Kitty's advantage with Mr Rosewood, there she saw her meandering through the fields, not too distant from where they were. Willow thought, since when does Kitty go for walks? Unfortunately, it was not even a moment before Mr Rosewood recognised her too.

CHAPTER 5

"Look there, Miss Philips, there goes Miss Richards. Come, let us walk towards her." So, he led Willow onwards, mostly pulling at her arm to walk faster.

By the time they reached that elegant and lithe figure, Willow's face had been clouded by an overarching sense of jealousy, especially roused by Mr Rosewood's enthusiasm for seeing Kitty. They exchanged general greetings, with Kitty offering an extra cordial 'Good morning' to Mr Rosewood and Willow providing an extra bitter handshake to Kitty. She watched with jealousy as Kitty gave her supple hand to Mr Rosewood and as he held it to his lips. Willow was sure, or at least tried to assure herself, that he had only followed through because of Kitty's pressuring eyes.

"So, I see you've met Miss Philips," Kitty said with her perfectly inflected voice, which was able to communicate so much scorn in one simple sentence. She didn't even direct her gaze towards Willow, as though it were a burden enough to refer to her by name.

"We have met each other last night, Kitty," Willow addressed her directly, "and continued our acquaintance this morning."

"Is that so?" Kitty's eyes opened wider, with jealousy Willow hoped."Well, that is great," she added with a fake jolly tone, but one that was so well-executed that Willow knew would have deceived Mr Rosewood, "then we can both keep Mr Rosewood company during the dinner. I'm meaning to send out invitations very soon, so don't fret too much about it. But, you know, Willow dear, I have finally received that pair of stunning Venetian slippers that I had been pining for all month."

She put forward her foot for her companions to admire her slipper. It was true, it was a very exquisite slipper and, in comparison to Willow's dusty walking boots, it seemed heavenly. Well, Willow only wished she could have stomped on that dainty foot of Kitty's and ruined those precious Venetian slippers forever.

"Here and look," Kitty continued, for she was not done yet, "these earrings have also been made in the latest Venetian fashion."

She pushed back her silky curls for them to examine her emerald earrings. Again, it was true, they were beautiful, but Willow wished Mr Rosewood wasn't there, for she was ready to exit the conversation at any time now.

"And here, darling Willow, look at my bangle," Kitty held out her wrist for the two observers and there was the bangle, which matched her emerald earrings.

Before she could explain its origins, Mr Rosewood intervened, after casting Willow his laughing brown eyes and a small wink, "Let me guess, Miss Richards, they're Venetian?"

As Kitty flushed and cast Mr Rosewood a look of disbelief, Willow could not repress her laughter and very audible giggles burst from under her hand, which was pressed on her mouth tightly.

Mr Rosewood too shared in the laughter, but he felt obliged to apologise to Kitty.

Affronted, Kitty took back her arm and let out her malice on Willow by sneering, "I could lend it to you when I'm done with it, Willow, for I know you haven't anything of the kind."

"I've plenty, Miss Richards," Willow continued with an indignant tone, which she found the courage to do so from Mr Rosewood's act of loyalty, "However, I don't wear them for daily occasions like you. Why, I don't know how you do it at all, Kitty, wearing your decorations when just taking an afternoon walk."

"You ought to," Kitty returned with the same contempt, "but I believe such ornaments are not suitable for your daily chores. I, on the other hand, have the leisure to wear all the jewellery I may wish to wear. You see, Mr Rosewood, I am quite fond of jewellery and hair ornaments and all the like. You'll find plenty of ladies whose husbands are willing to shower them with such gifts and treasures, but they simply do not care and would rather live with wearing practical 'everyday clothes', or so they call them. When I am married, I shall never do that. Yes, never. I'll accept my dearest's gifts and wear them quite proudly."

After her speech, Kitty nodded her head with such fake deference that Willow struggled to contain another laugh, resulting in a half-suppressed giggle and burning glares from Kitty.

CHAPTER 6

"And I know for certain, Miss Richards, something else. If I were ever to marry, which may be possible, indeed,"

To which Kitty answered, 'To be sure' and Willow struggled with yet another laugh.

"Well, to put it simply, I wouldn't shower her with ornaments and jewels and the like. Why, I'd prefer her to be comfortable with plain attire. I'd rather her be better at managing the home economics rather than blowing the finances out on frivolous things. I'd like a lady who didn't care for those things and would be content in being her own country self—for I prefer a true and honest character than one filled with capriciousness and vanity."

"But Mr Rosewood, I must assure that you understand one thing. It isn't to say that I am vainglorious or capricious because I care for my general appearance. In fact, I think it is a lady's duty to ensure that she always looks her best and I believe that she should go to every length to ensure that her duty is fulfilled, just as she is expected to with her homely duties. Why cannot she reward herself by being bejewelled? And why should she refrain from pleasing others with her presence? I think it is especially important to convey a positive image of oneself these days, as other people are continuously judging everyone around them."

Willow was beginning to feel extremely bored with the whole subject matter at this stage and began to wonder just why this was so important to debate.

Kitty continued, "Mr Rosewood, I am very sorry if you were to think me vain, but not even that would deter me from fulfilling this duty and I am certain that there are other people, even in this small town, that share the same views as me. That is to say, my view is not singular but one that you will find is supported by ladies from esteemed families and of genteel birth."

Willow let out an involuntary sigh.

Kitty stared her down and added, "Perhaps Miss Phillips does not agree with me at this present moment, but I am sure that she will in a matter of time. For you see, Mr Rosewood, even Willow agrees that being simple just won't do for a social appearance, however she is comfortable with being simple when she goes for walks. Well, that is all very good for Willow because she does not walk in company, except for with Mr Daniel when he is not engaged or she is sometimes in my company in the odd occasion. However, I am continuously sought after and I cannot take a walk without someone coming to seek my company, so I must always appear presentable."

Delivered with such seriousness, Willow made sure she did not let out a breath of laughter or else that would be the end of her invitation to the Richards' dinner. She casually looked about her, played with the stones at her feet and awkwardly set her eyes about Mr Rosewood to see what he would reply with. How glad she was that the speech wasn't directed towards her! Where Mr Rosewood could find something kind to say, Willow would only aggravate the situation.

Mr Rosewood did reply, after a very short pause, in his friend-liest tones, reassuring both his companions that he was generally happy with both their views as long as they were happy. "Miss Richards you do know that I do not think you vain, in fact quite the opposite. Whilst I didn't take your point of view into consideration before, I will certainly in the future. Think of it not as a point of disagreement, but a point of enlightenment for me and you have helped me to achieve this."

Willow observed that he was quite the diplomat and there would be no chance of Kitty ever being bored with him if he continued to agree with everything that she said. She was pon-dering this when Kitty's addressing her brought her back into the situation.

"Well, Willow, I should be off now in the opposite direction to you and Mr Rosewood I presume. But before I forget I would like to tell you how I am doing my hair on the night and how many other young ladies will on the night as well. That is, I've gathered this information from yesterday's house visiting. Well, everyone is going to have their hair done up high and mine will be of memorable height, so I'll just like to hint to you the current mode since I know you don't pay particular attention to these things. Now, I hope you'll take that into deep consideration, Willow and I'll speak to you about it soon, to be sure. I'll see your round Willow and adieu Mr Rosewood for now."

With the goodbyes exchanged, Willow was delighted to be walk-ing alongside Mr Rosewood once again with no Kitty to bother them. As soon as they were a considerable distance away from them, Willow sighed loudly.

"She's a handful, isn't she? Quite opinionated." Mr Rosewood said.

"Well, Miss Richards was always that way; I don't ever remember her being any less opinionated than what you've just witnessed if not more. Why, this is only the beginning, you haven't heard the least of it." She checked herself. "That isn't to say that she's not a lovely person." Willow added under her breath, "Well, she could be if she really wanted to."

Mr Rosewood heard her mutterings and laughed. "I think I'm beginning to understand your situation, Willow. I think I'm beginning to understand why there seems to be some tension between the two of you. It would really be wonderful if she would only be a little more courteous, but I'm afraid that she isn't quite ready for your modern sort of thoughts."

"Modern? Kitty believes that she knows of all things ancient, classical and modern, you should never bring those up when you're with her. Oh, how she'll talk of things that you'd never heard before with her obscure Latin terms and loaned foreign words. Well, she even outdid me in a conversation about flowers. Flowers! Think about how utterly random that is and you'll be surprised how many words she knows. Never," she added between laughter, "ask her about flowers."

"I'll certainly make sure that I won't, especially since I've no knowledge on flowers. Although, I'd like to think that I am patient enough to bear it through." He smiled that friendly smile of his and Willow wished she could push him into reality away from his rose-tinted view of the world.

"Well, I'd admire you if it were true." What else could she say to him without making offense? She shifted the basket to her other hand and looked out at the horizon, bare with scattered trees reappearing every now and then.

CHAPTER 7

It was early afternoon and the sun was especially strong on this day. The sky was a clear blue with those rare, white clouds appearing in isolated blotches all around. Alongside the gravel path they were walking on, were trails of different coloured stones arranged there by the school students on their field trips; there were dark grey stones, brown stones and red stones, which matched the colour of the land in the distance. Willow was so intently looking down at the gravel path that it took her a while to realise that they were not walking towards her home, but instead entering the park.

"And I see that we're going to take a walk around the park are we?" She turned to her left to study his profile; as handsome as it was a few days before in the moonlight, only slightly more golden now that he was under the blazing rays of the sun.

"Of course if you don't mind. I think the sun is only getting fiercer and a nice cool walk under these trees should provide us with some refreshment. Are you willing to go for a walk?"

"Why not, I guess I don't have too much to do today anyway." She freed herself from his arm as soon as they entered the park, as she was intending on picking some flowers, but Arthur was quick to reject this.

"Please don't let go of my arm, Willow. Not now, I'd like to have it with me—"

Whilst Willow would usually fall to his kind biddings, she knew that the line was drawn at false statements; how could Arthur be so attached to her in such little time? She attempted to check his behaviour, "I'd like for you not to hold on to my arm since I'd rather enjoy its freedom and pick some flowers."

"But then," as he began speaking his lips curled into a devilishly imposing, cunning smile that Willow had never noticed before, "you know that Kitty will be watching us strolling through here? And that she'll be standing on the top of one of those hills, looking at us specifically? Wouldn't you like to give her the impression. . .?"

She interrupted, "No, Mr Rosewood I would like to do no such thing. If that is the only reason that you have asked me to walk with you, I think that it is fair for me to be offended in some way. I will not hold your arm for that reason and if you aren't happy with that, then you're more than welcome to leave me, as I am more than capable of making my own way home as I always do. You shouldn't be under the pretense that I am so attached to your presence." Willow couldn't bear to look at him because while she did actually want him to stay, she couldn't let him think that she was a tool for him to provoke Kitty's jealousy with, no matter how much the young lady deserved it.

Rather taken aback by the assertiveness with which he was replied, Arthur gave his apology and strived to make himself as agreeable and obliging as he could for the rest of the walk.

As the two kept on walking, it took only a minute or so for Arthur to prove himself worthy of Willow's arm again. The gentleman did not have to wait much longer for the two to be walking side by side, with Willow on talking terms with him once more, as she had previously decided to keep her responses to his general questions rather brief.

"And when do you think your friend Charles will be returning from his trip to the city?" Arthur asked Willow at one point.

"I think sometime after the Richards' dinner," Willow replied, staring fixedly at his face for any clue of the reasons behind his asking.

"Well," he smiled discreetly to himself this time and his brown eyes sparkled brightly as he moved his face up into the sunshine, pretending to be surveying the lorikeets in the trees, "that means I won't have to worry too much about any competition for your company on the night."

Willow would have coloured, but she had too much determination against it that she seemed coolly unaffected by his playful jests. "I wouldn't say so if I were you, Mr Rosewood, there are plenty of other young gentlemen."

"No, I won't bother about them; I can outdo the whole bunch put together," he laughed and shook his wild curls about, sending them jostling about his face, Willow was sure this was a self-conceited laugh. "No, it's this Charles that I worry about who has won your esteem."

"I've known Charles for much longer than I have known you; a hundred times over. So, you shouldn't be comparing yourself to him, Mr Rosewood, and I wish you'd stop talking in this way because it really pains me to be constantly on the defense and it makes me wish that you'd only be quiet like this rose I have here in my basket. See, you're nearly as beautiful as it is (mind you, don't smile to yourself, I said nearly), but you're nowhere near as peaceful; you bring me such headaches, you do."

Not heeding the warning he was given, Arthur inwardly smiled to himself and looked at his companion warmly, as his face softened into a look almost fuelled by admiration, but mostly propelled by playfulness. "You've just compared me to a rose, Willow. I think I ought to consider you won over. There, I did it, under a week!"

"Don't be so joyful, you haven't done a thing. Say something like that one more time and you'll be sure never to catch me complimenting you again." But her delivery was far from serious, as Arthur's piercing eyes looked straight into her rather than at her, and she felt herself to be lost in his uncommon charm.

CHAPTER 8

A week passed until the night of the Richards' dinner, and it would have been an understatement to say that the young ladies of the community were excited about the number of young gentlemen coming to the event and even the opportunity of making the acquaintance of Mr Rosewood. In the leading hours to the dinner, everyone was preoccupied in their own personal dress and appearance, ensuring that they were suitably dressed, especially those lost young ladies who held such hopeless admirations in Miss Richards and who would esteem her opinion over that of an actual respectable lady, if they were to be introduced to one.

On this night, perhaps Willow fell into this category, although she never at once thought that she had. For was she not taking Kitty's advice about how to do her hair? And was she not trusting the information that had been given to her by one of the people that she liked the least? Well, Willow never at once thought of this because, simply and honestly, it was all aimed to gain the attention and preference of the charming Mr Rosewood. Despite any claims that Willow would make against these or any vain denials, this was the truth; and inside, Willow knew this was true, but she did not seem to control those feelings within her that made her aim to be noticed by this particular person.

It might not have been all in vain, for, after all, Mr Rosewood would not have shown such an interest in her if he did not actually feel that way. And that time when they had met with Kitty, he had tried to take her own side, and was that not an early sign of loyalty? Willow thought so and was turning over all of the wonderfully kind things he had said to her, and the warm looks he would cast on her, and those sweet, friendly smiles of his. However, she must enter into this even with a clear head, with no expectations of his behaviour or their interactions at all. How could she predict if he would suddenly cast her in the cold and prefer Kitty? After all, his behaviour could very well be liable to changes in front of other people and this she could not know, since all of their meetings had been in informal settings.

Yet, Willow retained some hope that he would treat her with the same warmth and kindness as he had done all those other times. So, hope she did.

Willow and her mother had settled on walking to the Richards', as it would have been too impractical to go in any other manner but on foot. Sure enough, many others had the same idea and there were a group of ladies entering the house before Willow and her mother. Kitty's family home was a neat farm villa, rather grand for the locality that it was found in, it was made to resemble a sort of Federation style of their old residence. In the doorway, they were greeted by Mrs Richards, cordially, and Willow continued on with that puzzle that had perplexed her for years; how could it happen that such a kind and hospitable lady could be Kitty's mother?

Such mysteries are never for any of us to figure out and Willow soon found herself casting her eyes all about the drawing room for any sign of Mr Rosewood, but for a few minutes she could not find him. So, she followed her mother around, talking to the people she talked to and trying to pay attention to the conversations, which to Willow did not have any importance, as she was sure that even the smallest exchange of words with Mr Rosewood would make her happy enough for the whole evening.

And that is how she found herself listening, half grudgingly, to a conversation about curtain colours and which style would be best in the modern drawing room.

Willow, looking around, could see many young ladies and gentlemen, but no sign of Kitty, her friends, or Mr Rosewood. Not being able to stand another question about curtains, Willow waited to make the best exit from the conversation and began to move away from the drawing room into the antechamber, which, due to the capacity of people, was being used as an extension of the drawing room.

She only stood at the entrance of the room, near the door, and the first person she saw was Kitty, with her hair in low swooping curls, facing away from her and, opposite of her, Mr Rosewood was standing. Willow did not move behind the wall fast enough for Mr Rosewood not to see her, in fact, he had caught a glimpse of her distinctive ebony black hair made up in fancy ringlets on the top of her head. Although Willow could have easily made her escape into the next room, she waited, perhaps thinking that Mr Rosewood would leave his conversation to come and greet her.

In her hopes, she had been lingering for about three minutes in the drawing room, not too far away from the anteroom, expecting him to appear at any second, but he never did.

It felt like a long wait to Willow until dinner was served and even then, she thought that there was still hope in him coming to greet her. But for every second that passed, Willow's anger grew, until she was quite determined that if he did come to speak to her, she would be as curt as possible.

CHAPTER 9

To her relief, she saw that her seat had been placed, most probably by Kitty, on the other end of Mr Rosewood and Kitty's place on the table. However, she caught Mr Rosewood talking to Mrs Richards softly and pointing over in her direction. With too much pride, Willow made sure not to make eye contact up until Mrs Richards came to her. The gentle woman came to her and told her that Mr Rosewood had suggested that her seat should be moved nearer to that of Kitty because he was aware of the friendship between the two. Although unimpressed by Mr Rosewood's actions, Willow tried to be as courteous as possible when accepting the change.

She passed the dinner sitting opposite of Mr Rosewood and next to Kitty who, with her fake laughter and snide comments, sometimes made Willow feel like unwinding the spaghetti from her fork and using it to poke Kitty's arm. She tried not to say a word against Kitty and, to her own personal satisfaction, Willow did not utter a direct sentence to Mr Rosewood, only answering through Kitty, much to the lady's delight.

After the dinner was cleared, many people left soon after, but the rest of the company moved into the study. Willow made sure to remove herself from her mother and her friends, who were still on the subject of curtains, and found herself a neat window-seat at the very end of the study. There she had the leisure of watching everyone, whilst being herself concealed by the curtains.

She sat there for about half an hour, watching Kitty talking to Mr Rosewood and the other girls with various high-hairstyles about her Venetian curls that were arranged at the bottom of her head. Despite knowing that such frivolous things should not matter, Willow was annoyed, very annoyed. And the current situation with Mr Rosewood did not help at all.

There he sat, on the divan, looking up at Kitty, quite breath taken by her beauty, or so Willow thought. But, to Kitty's discontent, he could not be entertained by talk of Venetian fashion for too long, after a session of ten minutes, he had gotten up to walk to the other end of the study, towards Willow's window, to speak to some gentlemen.

Willow shrank back within the window and pulled the curtains a little more towards her, this time hoping that he would not come to speak to her, as she had nothing kind to say to him. Her eyes were fixed on him for a while and she watched him as he talked animatedly, with arms and body swaying and moving with such cool and collected passion. That golden brown face of his seemed to sparkle tonight and Willow thought he looked most becoming in his sharp vest and trousers, but the deep, dark eyes only brought Willow more anger. Those eyes had no attention for her tonight, as she had hoped, but for another company of ladies.

She turned towards the window and began looking outside. From there, she could see the park where they had walked together about a week ago and, at that time, she recalled him to seem so happy to be in her presence. She focussed on particular trees and houses for around two minutes at a time and was hoping to continue this until it was time to leave or she ran out of things to look at out the window.

Just as she was getting bored of looking out the window, she felt the warmth of another person sitting by her on the window seat. She knew before she turned her head that it was Mr Rosewood; could it be true that she was now able to distinguish his warmth? Willow was beginning to think so.

He smiled, half-pityingly, as he looked about her little refuge, "You've made yourself rather at home here. I've been keeping a watch on you for the past hour and you haven't even stepped out."

Willow didn't even bother giving him a reply, she was too affected at this point to speak coolly.

"Anyway, I'd like to tell you that you've been rather cold to me this evening, ever since dinner time. What's wrong?"

What's wrong? Willow thought, Oh, I'd tell you what's wrong if I didn't have to be polite. And what, I'm being cold? Were you not the one who completely ignored me? She would have liked to have replied.

He paused, searched her face with his peering brown eyes for an answer, and seemed to have found one. "So, it's about earlier tonight? I apologise that I didn't follow you into the drawing room to greet you, I was held up."

She unfolded her arms and was beginning to speak, but he placed his hand on hers, that was lying in her lap. Willow was quick to cast his hand away and placed hers decidedly behind her back.

"Oh, don't be like that. You know," he began whispering and leaned closer, "you know how Kitty is, she wouldn't let me go anywhere. Come, Willow darling, you'd understand?"

"No, I don't. And don't call me 'Willow darling' when you've just ignored me for the whole night, it doesn't add up and it makes you seem hypocritical. Now, Mr Rosewood—"

"Now it's my turn; don't call me 'Mr Rosewood' when you know you can call me Arthur."

"Fine. Arthur," Willow enjoyed herself addressing him in that way, but was quick to resume her former tone, only giving him the chance for a momentary smile, "I wish you would leave me alone."

CHAPTER 10

He paused. "Are you sure? If you say so, I will just leave—" He started to get up.

"How awful of you! If I told you to leave, it means that you should. Why would you taunt me like that? Sit back down now." She exclaimed in hushed tones, "You know that you've been treating me unfairly, especially when you've been saying that you feel such—"

"I never talked about feelings," he sat back down, gave a sly smile and then broke into laughter, which continued increasing in volume, as he reacted to Willow's terrified face at drawing a crowd, only attracting the momentary attention of the whole study and the sneering stares of Kitty and her friends. "I'm sorry, I'll try and hush."

"You are only trouble, you know. Right now, I could almost wish that I had never taken such a liking to you. You said you would like to be my friend and I was more than willing, but right now, I can't see that you're acting so friendly. Actually, having thought it over, perhaps it would be better that you'd leave me. Go, didn't I tell you to leave?"

"Yes, and when I was leaving you told me to stay." He chuckled, "Don't you see—"

'Don't you see that you're mean to me? How could I let you go when you're smiling at me like that? If you keep that up, I don't think I'll ever have the strength to get you to leave." She paused and brought her hands back into her lap. "Why are you staying here with me? You can go back to Kitty and those girls. I'll definitely get the cold shoulder for a whole month because of this."

"What do I care about Kitty? She isn't half of what you are." Arthur stretched himself out and lounged back, leaning against the window.

"Don't speak like that. You obviously think her to be superior to me and you can't deny that. What I wonder is why you even bother with me. Is it just to make Kitty jealous?"

He didn't seem to be affronted with the question, as Willow was hoping. Instead, he just smiled to himself and looked down when speaking, "I knew that would come up at some time, but never so soon. I don't know how you can think that. But, I guess that you don't trust me all too much. I mean, we've never met before these two weeks or so and you must think that I'm so strangely friendly to everyone. Although, I had hoped that you would understand."

There was a pause before he continued, "Well, I guess it'll come to you soon. That is, that I'm honestly an amiable person and I don't mean you any harm. I would never do such a thing to you or any other young lady."

"Alright, maybe you're right. But I still don't forgive you, just so you know." She tried to hide her smiling, but like every other time, he was too quick for her.

"It'll take quite a bit for you to like me again?" He nudged her with his elbow. "No, I don't think so. You find me exceedingly charming. Now, don't shake your head. I can tell by the way that you look at me. You should be happy that I'm acknowledging this and not using it against you. All the same," he put his hand in his waistcoat pocket and pulled out a little book, "this is for you. I hope you like it, I was meaning to give it to you later on, but I don't think I can keep it a secret any longer."

She took it from him and saw that it was a small and compact copy that was neatly bound and had elaborate decorations on the cover. She read the title aloud, "The Science of Botany: A Guide to the World's Native Plants. Why, thank you, Arthur, it's so kind of you. How should I thank you?"

"Well, that smile of yours is thanks enough. But, a handshake will complete it." He took her outstretched hand and shook it cordially. "Now, there we go. I found it that day we were in the book shop."

"Thank you, I'll enjoy reading it. Although, I think we've caught the attention of Kitty. What, already time to sing? Well, I think I'll just have to let you go and we'll see if you're really good enough."

With one of his playful laughs, he asked Willow to stand and take his arm and he accompanied her to the middle of the room where he then left to take his place by the piano next to Kitty. Willow took a seat on the sofa towards the left hand side of the piano, so that she could see Arthur's face directly and as little of Kitty's as possible.

One of Kitty's friends, Cecilia, shrilled with her merry voice, "Oh, do play something for us, Cathy, and I'm sure Mr Rosewood would love to join."

CHAPTER 11

So the singing was begun. Kitty played very well, her fingers moved fluidly up and down the pianoforte and her expression was marvellous. That merry musical introduction to the country ballad suited Arthur's cunning smile and his relaxed style of standing, as he laid one arm on the piano and the other hand was placed smartly on his hip. If it were anyone else, Willow was sure it would have been a ridiculous pose, but because of his unique charm and grace, it seemed as the most comfortable resting position.

Kitty began to sing and her voice was, as always, perfectly inflected, rising to high notes and soaring through them and not struggling with the low ones either. Her register was much more extensive than Willow's and her voice held such emotion and passion in it, that it surpassed all mechanical school-trained voices like Willow's.

Sure enough, when Mr Rosewood joined in, his voice was beyond exceptional and beyond anything that Willow was expecting either. His rich, deep tones reached to the bottom of her heart and struck cords within her, as she had explained the phenomenon to herself later on. By now, Willow had ceased looking solely at Arthur, as she felt herself to be incapable of staring at him when he was purposely fixing his eyes upon her too.

She had recalled that time when he mentioned he would be singing a love ballad, and now she had understood his meaning. It was all on purpose, to make her feel this way. Mr Rosewood knew that Willow would be overwhelmed by emotion if he sang a ballad especially to her. However, this knowledge was not only specific to Willow and Arthur, but the rest of the company also began to note this intense staring between the couple and whisperings had started around her.

Kitty tried to gain Mr Rosewood's attention by performing greater tricks with her voice; her voice was truly like an athlete, or so Willow thought, performing vaults and jumps, only to gain the attention of her audience, which in this case was only Mr Rosewood.

As they sang the last verse, Willow looked up once again and her eyes met his. And as he sang, Willow could feel herself burning up and the only thing she could afford to do was to continue looking at him and listen intently to the words:

Yet, what could he do, the poor farmer's son,

But sit yonder under that tree?

Waiting and watching for his sweet Marion,

Wild, willowy and free!

Of course, Arthur was bold enough to address that last line to Willow directly and a good deal of whispers followed after the song had concluded. Immediately after bowing, taking Kitty's hand and accompanying her away from the pianoforte, he threw himself next to Willow on the sofa.

"How'd you like it?" He sat as close to her as she would let him.

"To say that you were brilliant would be an understatement."

"There, and didn't I tell you you'd be amazed. Now, you know you were the person I was thinking of when I was singing, since the whole thing was addressed to you anyway." He tried to look into her eyes.

"You ought to stop that," she began to laugh nervously, curling her fingers in her skirts, "or you'll start a whole crowd looking at us. Besides, we already have Kitty and her lot observing us. And what's more, you'll make me blush and then they'll think all sorts of things."

"Why, let them think what they want." He shuffled closer so that he could speak softly into her ear. "Would you prefer going outside in the gardens? You can blush however much you want over there."

"Arthur," she held his arm down, as he was already half rising, "no, they'll make it—"

"Ah, the devil with them. Don't look at me like that; it's true." He pulled her up gently. "Let's go, whoever wants can follow."

She stood up after him and took his arm, "You're such a headache, Arthur. You should better leave me alone. I can't go outside, they'll all be thinking—well, and they'll be talking about us, thinking about me...and I so dislike being talked about. Now, please, I won't like you if you don't leave me."

"I think that the more you say you don't like me, the fonder our friendship becomes. Now, don't worry, I'll just smile at this gentleman here and that lady there, and we'll be out and into the garden as quickly as possible." He managed to pull her away from the sofa and through the crowd. Sure enough, people were whispering and others talking loudly, not caring if they were heard.

Kitty was watching them the whole time, exited the study, and stopped them in the corridor. "Mr Rosewood, why, where are you going?"

He stopped and turned. "Out on a walk with Willow. We're going to talk," he nudged Willow as he said this, as if here were actually saying to her, 'Just watch now'.

"Well, I'd like a walk, but I thought it would be too fresh outside, besides I didn't want to bother anyone since no one is as fond of walking as I am. But if I knew you were Mr Rosewood, I would have gladly come, you know, Willow doesn't like walking too much."

"Ah, so now you know what I like and don't like, Kitty? To be honest with you, you ought to stop behaving in that way because you aren't fooling anyone. If you think that will win any favours from Mr Rosewood, you're quite mistaken. Kitty it's time you show me some respect. You're not any better than I am." Willow reached a certain point where she was over anger, and the words came out of her mouth most naturally, but she was clinging on to Arthur's arm desperately.

He said softly and with a smile on his face, "You hear that Miss Richards, I agree with Willow. Your conduct isn't at all respectable. Now, if you please, we will go on and walk in the gardens. Maybe you could join us another day when you are more composed and haven't forgotten your manners. Au revoir, Mss Richards."

The two turned their backs on the immobilised Kitty and continued walking laughingly on towards the gardens. What a relief it was for Willow to finally understand whose side Arthur was on, but that still did not explain to her his previous incapability of giving her any greeting or being so overtly agreeable to Kitty. It was clear in her mind that she must still keep her guard, no matter how inexperienced she was.

CHAPTER 12

Arthur asked her once they were walking along the gravel path in the garden, "Now, don't you feel better in this clean air?"

The smell of dried flowers filled the warm, summer night's air.

"I'm certainly a little better, how about you?"

"I'll always feel great if I'm in your company because—"

"Ah, now, please don't Arthur, I'm not in the mood. Maybe another time—"

"What do you mean maybe another time?" He pulled her closer to his side, "Must I schedule specific conversations with you? My, you are a unique sort of person."

"If you like you can," she tried to smile discreetly, looking to the other side, "but, I can't guarantee I'll listen to you completely or believe you, really. I can't at the moment, not tonight."

"Whatever suits you is good enough for me, Willow. I'm not too worried about all that, but please let me talk to you a little more sweetly. It's as if every time I try to be— well, what's the word?—every time I'm trying to be sweet, you won't accept it. But I know you secretly cherish it, darling—"

Willow interrupted him amidst his great flow of words and removed his hand from her shoulder. "Don't do that Arthur, I'm telling you because I like you. It isn't helping you in any way. If you want to be kind to me, talk to me of things. Important things. Like you and me, not of sweetness... or other nonsense."

"Alright then." He paused. There was a silence for a few minutes in which neither talked, but they kept walking. Willow was relieved with the silence and found there to be a chance for relaxation.

Arthur began at length, "Well, I'm thinking of having a little group over at the mansion. Just an afternoon get together and then a picnic by the lake. What do you think?"

Willow hoped that that implied an invitation, but was not sure, so her reply was brief, "It seems lovely."

"I was contemplating on whether to invite Miss Richards. I don't feel like—well, you know how it is, but it wouldn't be very proper. But then wouldn't it make a point?"

"You should probably err on the side of caution. It wouldn't be very wise to exclude her, besides your acquaintanceship with Mr Richards has just begun and it must be very important for you, especially since you'd be looking at buying more farming land in the future. I'd be careful of not disappointing him, Kitty's his only child."

Arthur stopped walking, "Just how do you know about the land deal?"

"Well, I'm not entirely stupid if that's what you think. You've been so agreeable to Kitty thus far because of it, I've been thinking about it up until now and it was only tonight that I had pieced it all together." She paused and, to her disappointment, let out an involuntary, weak sigh that trembled as she spoke the first words,

"If I was right, that would also mean you'd intend on marrying her, and I don't see why not."

He took her arm again and began walking, "Look, Willow I can tell you quite confidently that if I ever was to marry, Kitty would never be in the question. I've told you before and I'm repeating myself now. Her country ways of boastfulness are so forced and her vanity impeccably—"

"What do you mean her 'country ways'? Do you mean to say that we're all so horribly spoilt here? Look, Mr Rosewood, I know you've travelled quite a bit and you've obviously earned the attention of more than a few beautiful, rich and eligible young ladies, but really? To downcast all of us here based on those stereotypical thoughts of yours, I didn't think that you were like that at all." She drew her hands across her chest and frowned severely at him.

"That doesn't include you, but it's true, everyone else is like that. How can I deny it? I see the truth, I say the truth. You can't expect me to do anything else about it Willow and if it is bothering you so much, don't ask me to leave again."

She looked at him with an eyebrow raised.

He continued, "I'll never leave you because I love your company. That's right; I've said it, even though you'll probably scold me for it. I can't be brought to leave you at all."

She opened her mouth to speak, but he interrupted her.

"If my saying the truth about anything annoys you, then I'll just have to tell you to leave me, if you have the heart to do it, but I know that you long for my company as much as I do. Although sometimes I do wonder whether you take me seriously at all, I must be just a town dandy or something rather frivolous in your eyes. Maybe if I were from around here, you'd take me seriously, as an honest man. Now, I've told you how I feel about Kitty and I know you might have been jealous... I don't blame you for it, but please don't think I'm speaking of you when it's actually her. Come, darling, don't be so."

And he pulled her arm with such tenderness that Willow had no other resort than to finally let herself trust him completely and wilfully let herself fall into his arms into a warm embrace.

CHAPTER 13

"There now! Don't you look lovely under this patterned moonlight in your blue dress?" He fixed up his vest and pulled her under the patchy shade of an old tree.

"Oh, the things you make me do, Arthur. I'm sorry; I never meant to insult you in that way." Willow threw herself into his arms again and hugged him tightly. Then she hesitated "But you don't mind me—I mean to say, it's quite alright for me to—"

"It's more than alright, my darling, come," and he embraced her tighter.

He leaned his back on the tree and held her body close with one arm around her back. With his other hand, he guided her hand to his chest and kept it tightly there.

"Arthur you need to know not to say things like that again."

"I promise you I won't, not a single word. It wasn't my intention to hurt you." He kissed her forehead. "Now, how about that picnic?"

As he was leaning against the tree, Willow could not help but stare up at what she thought was his wonderfully gorgeous face, which held that defined nose and she liked to think that his dark eyes held so much determination.

"I say you invite Kitty because," she paused, "well, I don't mean this to offend you, but you'd be giving up Mr Richards' friendship and any future business prospects."

"I wouldn't worry too much about those things. Let me worry about them. I don't think she'll be invited, but I doubt that means that she won't be coming."

Willow laughed, "What does that mean?"

"She'll find a way of inviting herself, certainly. I've known many people like her, gentlemen and ladies, with more money than she'll ever have, who behave exactly as she does if not worse."

Willow simply nodded and decided to sit herself down at the foot of the tree. Arthur promptly sat by her too and he started playing with the soil by his side.

They were both quiet for a while before Willow broke the silence. "Stop that Arthur, you're spoiling my dress. I don't want dirt all over it."

"Ah, that's no matter," he said as he crossed his arms on his chest, "but I'll stop anyway."

"This is my nicest dress, you see," she was shaking the fabric to get the soil off.

"You ought to have more," he leaned in closer.

Willow wished she didn't like it when he did that, but the truth was that she did indeed like it and she hoped he would only get closer. There was no way that she would let him know this, however.

"It's easy to say that I ought to have more, but it's another thing to afford these things." She laughed and let the fabric go, "They're horribly overpriced if you ask me."

Arthur didn't move an inch, he was still just as close. "It seems like a fair price to pay when you look so splendid in them."

"Oh no," she scooted away from him, "Arthur, I know perfectly well I look nice—"

"More than nice." He backed away with a downward glance.

Willow was shocked to sense a change in his behaviour. It was as if she almost saw him ashamed. He ought to feel so anyway, she reminded herself.

"But I'm sure you'd look even better without—"

And that feeling was gone. At least he stopped himself short, Willow thought.

Willow's cheeks coloured and while she knew that she should reproach him, she felt a part of herself dying to hear what else he was thinking.

She resorted to silence.

Recognising that he had inadvertently transgressed one of her boundaries, Arthur tried to make amends. He moved away from her even more and began to apologise. "I shouldn't have said that, forgive me."

She collected the skirt of her gown and moved closer to his side. Although she didn't want to say she forgave him, she definitely had accepted his apology.

Again, they spent some time in silence and Willow started looking around at the scenery. When it occurred to her to look back at the house, she caught the silhouettes of people standing by the drawing-room window.

"It seems like we've caught their attention." She sighed. "But what am I to do about it? I won't be able to stand their talk. It's not the old ladies I'm afraid of, but those silly young ones."

"Use it to your advantage, Willow," he started to smile, "they'd be dying to be in your position. What, with the richest young man that's ever come to spend time here liking only you? And, even better, him taking walks in the garden alone with you? You could teach them a lesson or two, and you should. Don't let them give you a hard time for being yourself. You didn't try to play any tricks on me as the rest of them did."

Willow was surprised to hear that. She asked with an eyebrow raised, "Tricks? What sorts?"

"Batting their eyelashes, talking sweetly and all that other nonsense that annoys me to the core because it is so hopelessly fake. But, let's not talk of it now—"

"It doesn't sound too different to what you've been doing to me, Arthur." Willow turned to look him directly in the eyes.

For a moment, she thought that he may have been offended, but she was pleased to see that he was only annoyed. That expression was soon masked by a smile forming on his lips.

She could only laugh in return.

"It seems I've been caught?" Attempting to appear unaffected by her remakes, he pushed back a stray curl and grinned, "At least it worked for a while."

"Oh no, Arthur, it never worked to begin with." She smiled back at him and began to stand up.

From the corner of her eye, she was watching his expression and she was glad to see him frowning.

"I think we should be getting back anyway," was all he could muster to say. He rose with her and they started walking back towards the house.

Willow began again, this time with a more serious tone, "Did you see how Kitty tricked me into doing my hair differently? Well, she just about tricked every girl into doing their hair this way, so she could look different to all of us. I ought to have suspected her of it, but I genuinely thought was being nice with her advice."

"It's no matter because I like it this way all the same." He took her hand and pressed it to his lips softly.

Perhaps now things are changing, Willow thought to herself.

CHAPTER 14

A week after the dinner at the Richards house, Willow had heard from her friend, Charles, that he should be home in the following days. His message was conveyed in such a fresh and hopeful tone that Willow did not at first realise the underlying confusion.

While he superficially tried to convey some sort of fondness for Kitty, Willow could sense that there was another meaning beneath these words. As a person that was inclined to consider all possibilities of any situation, no matter how improbable they might present themselves to be, Willow was preparing herself for the best news; that some time amongst fashionable society had led her friend to see Kitty in a different light. What she wasn't expecting, however, was that her friend would have found another young lady to attach his fondness to.

In the days following the Richards' dinner, Willow had tried to keep herself away from Arthur's company, only to be able to study his behaviour towards Kitty. This task was a rather difficult one to carry out, especially as she noticed that the more she kept away from Arthur, the harder he would try to find an opportunity to be with her.

Could she stop him from displaying his fondness for her so publicly? No, she could not. But, did she want to?

On a sunny Saturday morning, Arthur and Willow were attending the same garden party. This time it was Kitty's friend, Cecilia, who was hosting an event to try out her luck in winning over Arthur.

Although Cecilia's family did not have the same wealth as Kitty's family, she was determined to at least have a chance. All of the young ladies were invited, and all came, except for Kitty who denied the invitation with the excuse that she had an extremely important dress-fitting for a new set of autumn town clothes.

Whilst everyone was puzzling over the fickleness of the excuse, Willow knew in her mind, perfectly well, the real reason why Kitty did not attend the garden party.

Willow knew very well that Kitty detested Cecilia and there was a mutual dislike between the two girls. As such, Willow was sure that Cecilia knew very well that Kitty wouldn't have dared to attend her garden party.

Having been former friends of the two, Willow knew that Kitty disliked Cecilia's penniless state and, being as contemptuous as she was, Kitty did not let an opportunity pass where she could remind Cecilia of her inferiority.

But all the better for Cecilia! For she was beaming at the prospect of having Mr Rosewood's attention. Yet, she knew that Willow stood in her way. So, Cecilia and her mother (for she too was just as fixed as her daughter on the idea of marrying into wealth) made quite a hole in Mr Johnson's wallet to pay for the expense of this party. Even for country standards, it was not absolutely sophisticated, but it was not mediocre either.

Willow knew, from the snippets of information she heard when her mother's friends were gossiping, that the Johnsons did not have any money at all. In fact, she remembers very well that not too long ago they were forced to sell some land and all but one of their carriages.

During the day, Willow was standing in a circle near her hostess' daughter, trying to make herself as amicable as possible and hoping that Arthur would not make a sensation over her when he finally arrived, for he had a habit of making late appearances to any social event he attended.

Cecilia was not very open to Willow's friendliness, but as they talked she began being more amiable herself. Willow thought that the presence of three other young ladies was what helped. So, the two got on along quite long as they stood somewhere on the green lawn of the gardens under a shade of a flowering tree.

The group spoke of general things, that did not particularly interest Willow, but out of her fear of being treated as a competitor by Cecilia, she spoke with as much general interest as possible when speaking in a general manner about general things.

However, the generality of the whole situation was starting to bore Willow and soon enough she caught herself being annoyed and desperately waiting for Arthur to arrive.

I'd rather just sit in the house all on my own, Willow sighed as she plastered a superficial smile on her face. Arthur's probably enjoying his time off somewhere else, who knows? He's positively awful for leaving me bored like this.

She was interrupted by Cecilia pulling her arm, "Do you think you would like to make a page for me in my scrapbook, Willow?" She led her away from the rest of the group. "You can leave me some water colourings of the plants and flowers you like since I hear that you are so wonderful with botany."

"Well," Willow began, rather perplexed by the girl's friendliness, 'I'd be more than happy too." And as she faced the beaming smile, she felt compelled to add, "And perhaps you would like to add to mine after I've done yours."

"Oh, yes, please. That would be grand." Cecilia led her to a tea table with two chairs. She sat on one herself and signalled for Willow to take the other. "We'd make such wonderful friends."

"Yes, I'm sure." Willow stared blankly into the space in front of her. How long could she keep up this empty talking? She thought to herself, Why won't Arthur come already?

"Oh Willow, I hope you don't mind me taking the liberty of acting like a friend right this minute."

Willow replied she didn't mind at all but mumbled a small curse under her breath. How fake this whole thing is!

Cecilia didn't heed her mutterings. "I'd like to introduce you to someone. He's just in from town."

Willow was taken by the arm once again and led to another small group of people, this time a mix of ladies and gentlemen, on some other end of the green lawn.

She could see that she was being led to a careless looking young man who was wearing tennis clothes. As they neared, Willow recognised his face.

Willow began to feel that she had been too trusting in Cecilia; was this all a trick to drive me away from Arthur for this occasion? She was beginning to think that it very well was.

Cecilia began speaking, "Willow, you remember my cousin Rupert?"

The memories came back to her. "Yes, how could I forget?"

CHAPTER 15

Willow was trying to conceal the fact that she was annoyed from Rupert, after all, it wasn't his fault that Cecilia was trying to get rid of her.

As Willow looked at him, she noticed that he seemed to have changed from the last time she saw him, despite it being not that long ago. Ever since Rupert had graduated from boarding school, he had been alternating his residence between city and country. Willow remembered that the last time he had come to the country was almost three years ago.

"Willow, it's nice to see you again," Rupert said.

She smiled in return.

"Well," Cecilia had a smile on her face, "I think the two of you will have a splendid time catching up. I hope you don't mind me having to leave you for a little time now Willow, I think my mother needs me." And she went off, walking faster than Willow had ever seen her walk.

Annoyed, but attempting to maintain an air of calmness, she turned to face Cecilia's cousin. "So, it's been a while, Rupert. How are you doing?"

He played with the hem of his shirt and eyed her from head to heel before replying in a low, laughing voice, "I'm not too bad myself Willow. And yourself?"

"Just as well as I could be." there was something curious about the way he looked at her, but Willow couldn't quite catch what it was.

"Care for a stroll?" He offered his arm.

Willow took it without saying a word. If this was going to be an awkward conversation, she might as well stretch her legs.

"What brings you back here, Rupert?"

"Oh, you know how it is with me," he grinned, "I've had enough of the city. I might stay here for a while."

"Of course," she smiled, "you're always back and forth, and you never bother to tell me when you'll be back. You ought to write to me, you know? Charles always writes."

"Yes," he looked down at his shoes, "you're right."

"Anyway, you've come at the right time. The weather's been so lovely, and I think even though summer's ending it will be warm for a few more weeks."

"I'm lucky in that way, aren't I?"

They walked on, away from the clusters of people until they were quite removed.

Rupert asked to get her attention, "Willow?"

"Yes?"

"I'm not one to pry in any kind of girlish mess. Although, I must say, if it were not for Cecilia, I wouldn't have agreed at all. But I would rather tell you at once anyway. If my judgment of you is correct, Willow, you're a sensible sort of person—"

She interrupted, "I'm pleased you think so nicely of me, but I wouldn't say—"

"But," he was determined to continue, "well, I hope you don't take this to heart. I only dare to say it because we've known each other since childhood, despite not having seen much of one another lately—"

"What is it, Rupert? Really, I can take it." Willow was beginning to feel annoyed at him too. She was beginning to think that attending this garden party was a mistake and a waste of her time.

"I mean to say that you can be very competitive, and it can sometimes seem to others as jealousy—"

"Rupert," She stopped walking and took a step back in surprise. It seemed odd to her that the young man standing in front of her, which she last saw three years ago, was talking to her about her character.

"Please don't be offended," he moved in front of her and took one of her hands in his.

"What does this have to do with Cecilia?"

"I'll tell you now," he dropped her hand, "Cecilia's quite set on marrying Mr Rosewood. Don't tell her that I told you or she'd damn us both—pardon my language—" He let out a small laugh.

"I don't know how she got this into her head or how my aunt is letting her embarrass herself in such a way, but she thinks this garden party will help her. And, as you are well aware, you just happen to be her obstacle. Cecilia's a dreamy, childish kind." He sighed and shook his head.

Without a second thought, Willow nodded, but she soon caught herself, "I'm sure she's—"

"Ah, don't worry about it. I know it's true." He put his hands in his pockets, "Anyway, she thought that pairing you with me would stop Mr Rosewood from going after you today—so Cecilia could have a chance. She's also asked me to keep you away, you see."

"Oh, I see." It wasn't so much of a surprise to Willow.

"I'll tell you now that I won't keep you from him. You can do whatever you like, and I won't stop you."

Willow thanked him.

"But," he continued, rubbing his right arm with his hand, "if you'd prefer to stay with me, I think we'd have quite a lot to catch up on."

Willow had to stop herself from blushing, seeing him being bashful was such a fresh air from Arthur's straightforwardness that it almost led her to think that Rupert was interested in her.

"What do you say, Willow?" He asked again, but this time he was looking into the distance.

"I'd love to," she replied. "But first let me tell you how grateful I am that you have been honest with me." She offered her hand to him and shook his. "Honesty's a virtue that I find quite rare in those around me."

CHAPTER 16

It did not come as much of a surprise to Willow that Arthur did not make an appearance at the garden party. Something inside of her was telling her that Arthur would never show up. She was glad that she spent most of the party alongside Rupert. It had been a long while since they had spoken so intimately with each other and she had wondered that if he was not so often absent from their town, that perhaps there would have been something special between them. She found him to be more courteous and franker than she thought he was.

Of course, she thought, he isn't half as handsome as Arthur, but then she remembered that Arthur's handsomeness did not lessen his ability to annoy her. If only Arthur was as attentive as Rupert, she would have been sure that her heart would have been entirely devoted to him. However, that was not the case. Arthur continued to be a puzzle for her. She was not so sure where she should draw the boundaries and, very evidently, neither did Arthur. He played by his own rules when it came to feelings, yet he always had a way of making her feel safe and wanted.

One of the things that bothered Willow the most about her current situation was that she had no one to confide to. With Charles away, she was practically friendless, and while she could tell her mother snippets of information, she did not feel particularly comfortable in letting out the insecurities that troubled her mind.

Unluckily for her, she found herself this morning in the presence of her mother in their drawing room. There was nothing of interest happening that morning and Willow had decided not to seek out Arthur after his failure to show up at the garden party. She had preferred to stay home and speak to her mother on some of her issues, without revealing too much. They were sitting quite far from one another, Willow at the desk at the end of the room, and her mother by the window. Willow was working on Cecilia's scrapbook and making her some watercolours as she promised. Willow had to admit that she was rather surprised when Cecilia presented her scrapbook to her, she had never thought it was serious. Deep inside, she felt a little ashamed too.

"I dare say, Willow, you cannot think that your behaviour is completely acceptable," her mother had begun after a long silence.

"What behaviour, mama?" Willow asked as she looked up from the desk.

"Ignoring Mr Rosewood, I mean." She didn't bother looking up from her embroidery. "It is not right, dear, to make yourself so agreeable to someone and then, at the next minute, ignore them altogether. Does it not sound rather self-centred to you?"

Willow's cheeks coloured. She didn't like hearing her mother speak about her in a negative light, but she was thinking that perhaps her mother was speaking the truth. Willow hadn't stopped to think about her behaviour or Arthur's feelings. She simply had acted on her impulses.

Willow sighed, however much she did not like to think so, her mother was right. "I-I'm afraid you're right, mama. I don't think it rather adds up, does it? It must look so silly to you, but if only you knew..."

"Knew what, Willow?" She put down her embroidery. "You make it sound as if Mr Rosewood has done you wrong? If so, pray tell, but if not, I urge you to be careful. It also isn't right to make it seem as if one has done something that one has not."

"Oh nothing, he's done nothing. Only, well, only—"

"Not being at that garden party yesterday?" Her mother raised an eyebrow.

"Well, yes," Willow's voice lowered, "only that." She was beginning to see some of her foolishness.

"I do not think that is reason enough to treat him so." She laughed a little, "Come, do not look so gloomy, it does nothing for your face. What do you say I try to find us a way to be invited to dinner by Lord Rosewood and his wife?"

Willow started, "Oh no, that won't be necessary, mother." The last thing that Willow wanted was her mother going around trying to make herself amicable to Arthur's father.

"It would not be an issue, dear. You see Lord Rosewood and your father used to be quite close—"

"But mama, you know how busy father is and we couldn't possibly ask him to make the journey back home just for dinner."

"Nonsense, your father does not need to be here just yet, Willow," she smiled, "don't get too ahead of yourself, dear."

"No, no, no," Willow spoke quickly, her mother was getting too many ideas. "Nothing of the sort, mama. Just please, don't ask for an invitation just yet. I'll think of what you told me."

"Very well," she returned to her work, "soon enough."

Less than five minutes had passed before Willow caught her mother getting up to look out the window.

"What is it, mama?"

"It looks like someone is making their way here. How strange, I was not expecting anyone today."

Willow made her way over to the window as well and stood eagerly next to her mother. She could make out a figure on horse-back.

"It looks like a man I think," Willow said.

They both waited eagerly as the figure approached closer, so they could make out who it was. It was Willow who first guessed who the visitor was.

"Oh it's Rupert, mama," She could not quite decide if she was happy that it was him or surprised. She settled for a mixture of the two.

"Rupert? Rupert Johnson?" She turned to her daughter, "I did not know that the two of you were close."

"Neither did I."

"He must have liked your company yesterday," Willow's mother was smiling broadly.

"I suppose," Willow smiled to herself.

"Well, go fix yourself, child," her mother had been thrown into a frenzy suddenly. "Fix your hair, I beg you, and remove that apron, it only ages you." Then she stepped out of the room to tell the staff to invite their guest into the drawing room when he arrived.

Willow did as she was told and returned to her seat, where she tried to compose herself as naturally as possible. Her mother looked at her from the other end of the room and mouthed to her to continue working as she was before. So, Willow picked up her paintbrush again and pretended to make progress.

Then, the noise of the door being open by the staff was heard and they could hear their guest's footsteps towards the drawing room. Willow looked over at her mother and she seemed the most enthusiastic she had been in a while. It seemed as though her mother had just entered a new idea into her head.

Chapter 17

It was a while before the footsteps were heard by the corridor near the drawing room door. Willow was trying to look busy as her mother had instructed her, but she kept stealing glances towards the door. Finally, they saw Rupert standing by the door. He paused, smiled and entered the drawing room holding a bouquet of wild flowers. Willow's mother instantly rose and went to greet him. Willow could tell that her mother was pleased by Rupert's appearance. She could not deny it herself; he presented himself impeccably well. His clothes were obviously

Rupert approached Willow's mother first, he bowed his head. "It is a pleasure to see you again Mrs Fletcher. It has been a while since I have been in the country, but I had the pleasure of spending time with your daughter at the Richards' garden party yesterday." He turned to face Willow who was now standing behind her mother, and he smiled. "We had a most delightful time."

Mrs Fletcher looked at her daughter then at Rupert and smiled. Willow was worrying now more than ever that had mother's mind had already drifted to a territory from which there was no return.

Willow's mother began to speak, "I am very pleased to hear that you enjoyed her company. Why, Willow was just telling me this morning of how happy she was to have spent the afternoon with you yesterday."

Rupert smiled and stepped closer to the pair standing in front of him. Willow noticed the dimples in his cheek as he smiled and could not help but smile bashfully herself.

"I hope you would not mind Mrs Fletcher, but I have brought flowers for Willow." He extended his hand holding the bouquet towards Willow, "I saw them as I was riding and when I fixed my eyes on them I could not help but think of how suitable they were for you."

Mrs Fletcher stepped back and placed her hands on her chest. "Oh, no matter at all. Willow takes after me in that she loves wildflowers, and I always told her that a personally picked bunch of flowers will always be superior to any store-bought bouquet."

Willow remained silent and accepted the flowers from him.

"They are absolutely exquisite, you have wonderful tastes for a young man," Willow's mother remarked. "I ought to get one of the girls to put these in water, but they are so held up with work, I might just do it myself."

Willow recognised that this was her mother's way of excusing herself from the room, creating a respectable excuse for Willow to spend time alone with Rupert. She would have appreciated the action, but at the moment Willow was not so keen on spending time alone with him. She felt a voice in the back of her mind telling her that somehow this was not the right thing to do by Arthur, but then again, another side of her recalled the way he had continued to act with Kitty.

With as much of a friendly tone as she could muster, she said to Rupert, "As my mother said, Rupert, it was so kind of you to bring flowers and to pay us a visit."

"Yes," he stepped closer to her, "I was just riding, I didn't have an intention to disturb you and your mother this morning, but when I saw those flowers..." He started smiling again.

Willow thought he was being odd at this point. She thought that there was nothing so special about her that would warrant him being so suddenly interested in her.

"Well," he shook his head as if he was bringing himself out of his thoughts, "I already told you that before. So, that's what brings me here."

They stood there in the middle of the drawing room, Rupert on the brink of blushing and Willow feeling rather helpless.

"Oh," Willow started suddenly, "it isn't polite of me at all! Please, take a seat." She hurried over to the divan and gestured for him to sit on the armchair opposite.

He gave a small laugh and followed her request to sit on the armchair. Without saying a word, he smiled.

Willow felt lost and started looking down at her lap. Her mother was taking an awfully long time putting those flowers in water. She was thinking of what to say next, but all she could think of was the weather, so she resorted to remaining silent. She was wondering where this sudden awkwardness had come from, as she thought that they had a lovely time yesterday and their conversation moved so easily. Willow wondered if it could have been the novelty of the situation, she could barely remember the last time Rupert had been in her home and she did not recall him ever visiting alone.

It was not long before Rupert asked her, "I hear that Charles will be returning soon?"

Willow sat up and smiled, "Yes, we are expecting him any day now."

"I'll be glad to see him again," he leaned back in his seat, "and I'm sure you will be too."

"Of course, I'm sure you know that Charles and I—"

"Are as close as ever," he finished her sentence for her. "Yes, I know," he smiled, "it's been that way for many years, has it not?"

"Yes," she looked down and smiled.

He laughed to himself and Willow looked up at him again. He seemed to be in such a good mood, but Willow did not know if this was usual for him or not.

Rupert noticed her looks and leaned in to explain, "You know, ever since I returned I've been hearing bits of stories about out old Arthur."

"Oh," Willow was slightly disappointed. She did not want to talk about Arthur with him. "Yes, he's caused quite a stir, Rupert. I think it's because he's been quite a mystery to us before his arrival." She paused, "But you must know something more about him?"

"Yes, I'd see him and Lady Rosewood frequently," he spread his hands open, "they were everywhere." He laughed.

"Oh, I can see that," Willow laughed along this time too. His positivity was starting to be contagious. "He's so unusually friendly and open, I just don't understand it, Rupert."

Rupert's eyebrows jumped slightly, but it was enough for Willow to realise that she had let on too much information. "So, you've had the chance to be acquainted with him?"

"Yes, I have," was her brief reply. Then she added, so as not so seem curt, "He's every bit as refined as we all thought him to be."

To her surprise, Rupert relaxed and sank back into the armchair. "Yes, if only you saw how easily he was fitting in with high society."

"Oh, I'm sure, Mr Rosewood's quite the conversationalist," Willow drifted off into thought, "Sometimes I wonder how he can cope being so kind to everyone."

"It beats me too," Rupert joined her in her speculation, "although I've learned not to question it; it must be a part of his nature."

"And what a wonderful nature that is," Willow breathed dreamily. She gasped at her mistake and all that she could do was look up at Rupert and see how he took it.

Rupert just looked straight at her and smiled. She could tell he was trying hard not to laugh because of the way his lips were pressed and how he squinted his eyes.

She looked away from him and down at her shoes. "You oughtn't to look at me in that way, Rupert."

"I'm sorry," he looked away still smiling, "I shouldn't have."

There was silence and then Willow burst out laughing. She stood up from the divan and walked behind it still laughing. Rupert couldn't help but laugh along with her.

"Oh, dear," was all she could manage to say in the midst of laughter.

He stood up also and walked over to her, placing his hands on her shoulders once her laughter had died down. "I hope I haven't offended you, Willow?"

"Oh, no," she took one of his hands and held it in hers, "you could never, Rupert."

At that moment they heard footsteps coming nearer, followed by Mrs Fletcher's voice, "I heard so much laughter, something must be amusing."

Instinctively, Willow dropped Rupert's hands and walked around to the other side of the divan and sat down at her former seat just in time.

As she stepped into the drawing room, both Rupert and Willow looked over at Mrs Fletcher's and they saw a warm smile take over her face.

Rupert spoke first before she could, "I was just saying to Miss Fletcher how nice it would be to take a walk before the afternoon heat sets in."

Willow turned her head around to look at him standing behind her at the divan. He saw her from the corner of his eye, but he only smiled and paid her no attention.

Not wanting to look passive, Willow added, "Yes, mama, and I was just saying to Mr Johnson how much I would like to stretch my legs." He added, looking down at Willow, "Of course, Mrs Fletcher, with you as her chaperone."

She turned around again and looked up at him. This time he looked down, smiled at her and gave her the most indiscernible wink.

CHAPTER 18

The day after Rupert's visit, Willow was left thinking about the easiness which she felt when she was around him. Throughout their afternoon walk, Willow did not feel as though she had to be on guard, as she did when she was around Arthur. Their connection seemed to have roots in some old familiarity that was distant enough for the two to discover each other anew. However, with Arthur, there was always that charming effect that he had on her and Willow was always inclined to sturdy herself against this. The last thing that she wanted was making Arthur think that he had such an influence over her feelings.

With Rupert there were no such feelings. Whether this was good or bad, Willow was unsure. Perhaps it was due to the fact that her mother was acting as a chaperone during their walk that Willow felt such a strong sense of familiarity, or that his manners were so like what she was used to. There was no rebellion in Rupert and for that, at least, she felt grateful for. Sure enough, being with Arthur held that element of secrecy and excitement. Their private strolls through the fields, their meetings under the moonlight and stolen glances gave Willow such a thrill sometimes that she wondered how she could ever settle for anything mediocre. But, over time, Arthur's ways had led Willow to question if his intentions with her were serious. She had no doubt that he was noble, but whether he would ever marry her was a great question in her mind.

Yet, she could not feel right in avoiding Arthur for any longer. Some part of her needed to be around him, to see his earnest brown eyes sparkle as she looked up at him laughing, and to feel the warmth of his body as they walked arm in arm. So the morning after Rupert's visit, Willow was resolved to see Arthur. Her mind was made up, she would go to him. She would tell him how she felt and perhaps all this confusion in her mind about Rupert would disappear. Yes, she thought, that is the only way. She was most certain that her confusion would disappear once she was in Arthur's presence again.

After breakfast, Willow dressed in her usual walking habit and made off to the familiar field where she knew Arthur would be.

As she walked, she tried to put together some kind of introduction, but she found that the words were not coming to her easily, so she quickly dropped that pursuit. She would find the words when the time came and, even if they didn't, she knew there couldn't ever be an awkward conversation with Arthur.

She had not walked very far before she noticed Arthur's figure standing opposite a tree and talking. Willow realised he must have been talking to someone who was leaning against the tree. She backed towards a tree herself and stayed to figure out who it was. She was too far away to hear their voices, but she did not want to risk being spotted spying on Arthur.

To her surprise, she saw feminine arms looping themselves around Arthur's neck. It had hit her then, it could have been no other but Kitty.

Willow watched in shock as the girl placed her arms around him and caressed his hair. Arthur's reaction was to step back and remove her arms from around him. He looked confused and overwhelmed, she could see him nervously brushing his hand through his hair. Willow had never seen him in such a state before. Mr Rosewood, who was always composed and knew precisely what to say at any given moment, was now being overpowered by a young lady.

She was glad to see him turn and start walking away from the tree, but her heart sank once again when the woman began to follow him and got a hold of his arm. It was at that moment, when the tree was no longer obstructing Willow's view, that her guess was confirmed. Next, she heard Kitty's own distinctly shrill voice calling out, "Arthur! Don't leave me here like this."

Catherine Richards, she said aloud to herself, of course.

Willow made it a point to stay for longer and observe the couple, there could be no good in leaving at this point. She stayed until, to her relief, Arthur shook Kitty off of his arm and walked away. Willow made out that he had mentioned something to Kitty before he left, but his voice was not loud enough for her to hear. Kitty, remaining behind for a moment longer, looked left and right before she wrapped her shawl tightly around her body and made off towards the direction of her house.

Now Willow was faced with the direction of either turning back home or seeking Arthur. But what would she say to him if she did go after him? Should she tell him that she had seen what Kitty had done or should she wait till he mentioned it himself? If he mentioned it, she murmured to herself.

Leaning against the tree, Willow began to wring her dress in her hands. Decisions were not her strength. But, this was a time for a change, she had to be decisive from now on. She concluded that seeing Arthur right now was the only choice she had if she wanted to no longer avoid him.

Mustering up some confidence, Willow started walking briskly in the direction that she had seen Arthur leave.

As she walked through a bushier part of the field, she realised that Arthur must have been walking in the direction of his house. If that was the case, she figured she would have to be careful not to be seen. Their relationship had already transgressed many social rules and Willow could not bear for any real evidence of their impropriety to become known.

Thankfully, due to Arthur's slow pace, Willow was able to catch up to him before he reached the lawns of his own home. Noticing the sound of someone trampling behind him, Arthur turned around to find Willow.

She stopped in her tracks and started by saying, "Mr Rosewood, I came to—"

Arthur cut her off to correct her, "Please, Willow, you must call me Arthur." He came up to her and stopped when he was half an arm's length away from her. "Especially now more than ever do I need to hear you saying my name."

"Arthur," Willow sighed and inched closer to his body, "I know what happened. I saw it, I was there looking for you and instead. . ." She didn't bother to finish her sentence.

He wrapped his arms around her and pressed her close to his chest, "Willow. . . my own darling—". Then he sighed and distanced her with his arms, "I apologise, you've already spoken to me about my language. It's a horrible habit I have, I know. Not at all proper for an innocent lady like yourself."

Willow had to stop herself from hugging him once more. "Can we talk here, or would you prefer to go somewhere else?"

"I think we should retreat further out." He took her hand in his and led the way.

CHAPTER 19

They had reached an apple orchard not far from the edge of the Rosewood estate when Arthur took Willow within his arms. She could smell his flowery hair and freshly cleaned jacket. Strangely, she thought it was a smell she might associate with Rupert and not Arthur, but nonetheless, she was here to enjoy his embrace.

He let go of her gently once he felt her struggle for fresh air. With his hand, he caressed some stray strands of her ebony hair behind her ear. Willow could not help but let out a small gasp at the delicateness of his hand. It wasn't just that his fingers were soft, but it was the whole effect of his hand trailing tenderly across her temple and the look in his brown eyes that made Willow remember why she found his so irresistible.

Still, she reminded herself, he had to explain what that scene with Miss Richards was all about. She knew she might expect something of the sort from Kitty, but all that she needed to hear from him was that it was some sort of mistake.

As though he had read her thoughts, Arthur said, "I rejected her."

Stunned and interrupted from her thoughts, Willow seemed not to comprehend, "What?"

"Kitty—I mean, Miss Richards. I rejected her. She had come to..." He hesitated for a while and knotted his eyebrows tensely. "There is no pretty way of saying it, I'm afraid."

Willow noticed the tension in his shoulders and placed both her hands on either side of his neck and began to soothe him as best she could. Looking up at him in earnest she asked, "What are you speaking of?"

"I was extending the invitation for my picnic to her and, well, she had come to make it known," he paused to read Willow's expressions. Upon finding her quite at ease, he continued, "that she wanted me to propose to her."

The young woman's arms dropped from his shoulders. To be honest with herself, Willow was expecting Arthur to say something along those lines. After all, it would be the only explanation for the odd scene she had witnessed with Kitty extending her bare arms out to Arthur and calling after him. But it all did seem too real when she heard the words coming out from Arthur's lips.

"Truly?" Willow looked up at him.

"Truly," he replied cautiously. He had not the slightest idea how Willow would take any of this news. All that he knew was that he owed it to her to tell her.

"But why would she ask it of you so directly?" She placed her hands on his chest and began playing with his cravat.

"I believe she overestimated her power." He put his hands in his pockets. "From what I understand she thought that my father and I were so desperate to seal the land deal with Mr Richards that I would agree to marry her to make the process speed along. I cannot comprehend which logic she thought she employed when she thought that up."

"And what did she think would happen if you rejected her?"

"Naturally I think she didn't think that an option, but I'm sure she'll be out to meddle in whichever way she can."

To some degree satisfied with Kitty's imprudent behaviour, Willow smiled. "I wouldn't worry if I were you. Around here we all know enough of Kitty's silliness, I doubt Mr Richards would ever consider her opinion in anything."

Willow was all smiles, but as she looked up at Arthur she noted his worried face. There was something amiss. He looked like a child that had just been scolded. Then it occurred to her that she had not done her side of explaining and it must be so awkward for him to accept her warmth after all this time of her ignoring him.

"Arthur?"

"Yes, Willow."

"The reason I was there to see what happened was that I was coming to see you this morning."

He continued looking into her eyes. His mouth twitching slightly at the corners, Willow supposed it was either nervousness or he was contemplating whether to say something.

"I had come to apologise, Arthur." She stepped back. "I have been ignoring you because, to be honest with you, I've been confused. Everything I have been doing with you has gone against the upbringing I have had. Even being here with you isn't right, not without a chaperone at least." Willow tried her best not to look at him. "Yet, I still feel something when I am around you. I feel that it is right, even when I know that it shouldn't be. Your sweet talk worries me sometimes because I'm scared of my own reaction to it. Whenever a compliment passes your lips, I get thoughts that are too deep for my own understanding. Perhaps I should not be having these thoughts at all, but I love them. And," she was now bringing her speech to a close so she forced herself to look into Arthur's eyes, "I'm also scared by the secrecy of it all. If you feel what I feel, why not do it the proper way? Do you actually feel it too?"

This last question of Willow's was delivered with such a raw blend of confusion, sadness and hope, that Arthur had to grab a hold of her.

He brought both his arms around her waist and pulled her close, or rather, guided her closer as she quite willingly retreated into his chest.

"Oh Willow, if only you knew how I feel it too."

Willow replied, but her speech was muffled as her face was nuzzled in his chest, "Then show me."

Nonetheless, Arthur heard what she had said, and he knew there was nothing holding him back now. He gently lifted up her small chin and tilted his head just so that their lips would meet perfectly.

At that moment Willow was sure that he was not lying. Those familiar butterflies she felt under her skin whenever he touched her had now amplified. She felt a series of tingles travel down to her feet as her own small lips explored his full soft ones. Willow wondered at how inexplicably delightful it was to finally experience the moment she had fantasised about.

Arthur pulled away and gave a small laugh, "You believe me now?"

"Oh completely," Willow replied back, caressing his cheek. She let a finger trace the lips she had just been kissing. She knew they were attractive, but never had she thought they would have been so irresistible.

"And I promise you," he whispered, "I'll do the proper thing from now on. Make visits, call on you, send cards, and so on, I'll have it all in order."

Her heart beamed with joy, she now knew she could give her all to him without fearing what his true intentions might be.

"Perfect," she whispered back, "but for now, could we not do the proper thing?" She stood on her tiptoes to plant a kiss on his lips once more.

CHAPTER 20

The day had come when Arthur hosted a picnic at his father, Lord Rosewood's, estate. Every notable family with a daughter was in attendance, including Mrs Richards and her daughter. Willow wondered how Kitty had found the nerve in her to show up after how she behaved with Arthur. Although, Willow pondered, Kitty probably thought that not a soul except for Arthur knew. She contemplated whether she should say something to her when she spotted her standing under a tree with Daniel, who was a long-time crush of Cecilia's, but she thought otherwise. Kitty was in the middle of her revenge-seeking, especially after that garden party thrown at Cecilia's house to which Kitty was definitely not invited.

Willow resorted to standing by her mother who was now talking to her friend Mrs Caldwell and her daughter, Mary, who Willow could not stand. It wasn't just her nasally voice, but her overall obsequious attitude to Kitty. Honestly, Willow thought, she was no better than Cecilia.

She plastered a smile on her face and held her chin high, occasionally putting in a word in the conversation.

All she wanted to do at that moment was seek Arthur, but it was not time yet. They had already seen each other as he greeted each of his guests with his mother upon their arrival. However, that was not enough. Willow wanted him to hold her. Oh, and how it pained her to see the corners of his mouth curling into a smile and holding her gaze on those pink lips of his.

It isn't fair, she thought, that I should be denied his warmth.

But, she sighed, she knew she had to control herself. It wouldn't seem proper anyway for her to be seen going around looking for the hostess' son. She must wait for him to finish greeting those who were still arriving, and only then would he have time to mingle with the guests.

It was just at that moment that she was lost in her thoughts and had zoned out of the conversation going on in front of her, that she had spotted a man behind Mrs Caldwell walking towards them. For a moment she hoped it was Arthur, but as he neared she could make out the red tint in his sleeked back hair and she recognised Rupert.

Willow expected to feel an internal disappointment, but, strangely, she didn't. In fact, she almost felt the opposite. How could she feel so nervously excited about Rupert showing up?

As he neared, the other ladies saw him too and began to greet him. Willow felt so removed from the situation as if she was sitting back in an invisible audience and watching a scene unfold itself. She watched him in his bright brilliance, with his reddish hair and pale face, so different from Arthur's warm earthy tones.

Willow felt off guard. Was it an attraction she felt? Then she thought back to their first meeting at Cecilia's garden party, and then later when he called on her at her house with the flowers he had picked himself. Rupert was the last person Willow thought she could develop a girlish crush on.

The next thing she felt was her mother's elbow poking into her ribs, awakening her from her thoughts. Now paying attention, she realised Rupert was smiling directly at her.

Stammering, and guessing what he had asked, she said hesitantly, "I-I do very well Mr Johnson. The weather is splendid."

Her mother groaned, though not quietly to Willow's dismay, and she could tell Rupert was suppressing a laugh. She pieced together that she hadn't guessed what he asked correctly.

Rupert was always on the verge of laughter, but not the mocking kind, it seemed to Willow. She saw the gleam in his eyes and she couldn't help but blush. She employed her fan and covered her face. It wasn't her intention to seem flirtatious or coquettish, but that's what Mary Caldwell must have thought because she brought up her own fan and gave her a cold sneer.

It seemed like eons before Rupert replied to her, but Willow was glad he brushed off her blunder. "Yes, the weather is quite nice. Lady Rosewood's events never occur on a dull day. Say," he turned to Willow's mother, "I was thinking of accompanying Miss Fletcher on a round of these gardens. With your permission, of course, Mrs Fletcher."

Willow's mother turned to Mrs Caldwell before she gave her permission and cast the woman a look with raised eyebrows. Willow knew what it meant. Her mother was showing off that Willow was chosen over Mary.

She knew it wasn't the most refined of behaviours, but she also knew that was the way of the people she had grown up amongst. Although it did pain her to think that Rupert, with all his privileged education and mingling with high society, would have thought this behaviour to be silly. But then again, she figured that Rupert would be used to it anyway, having more recently spent periods of time in his native locality. Unlike Arthur, she mused. But since when did she care so deeply about what Rupert Johnson thought anyway?

Willow took the arm that Rupert offered to her and left the group of ladies with a mocking smile at Mary Caldwell.

She was surprised to hear Rupert's laughter when they were a few steps away.

"What?" She asked.

"That smile."

"What about it?" It hadn't occurred to her that before this summer, Willow Fletcher was not the kind of person that fought fire with fire.

He looked down at his shoes. Willow began to think that he did that a lot.

"It seems like Arthur has taught you a few things."

She drew her body a little further from Rupert. She remembered that discomforting feeling yesterday when she thought of Rupert's flowery smell while being with Arthur.

"I didn't mean it to offend." He said with a tone of regret in his voice.

Willow wondered at how in tune he was with her thoughts. "None taken, Rupert." She brought back a smile on her face and turned to face him. "I guess I've learned to stick up for myself."

He looked down at her and she could feel herself softening under the gaze of his green eyes. "I like that."

That's all he said, just three little words. But to Willow it felt like a lot more. She knew Rupert, admittedly, a lot better than she knew Arthur. Those three little words from this well-trained and well-educated young man were meant to mean so much more, and Willow was sure of it.

She should have gently let him know that she wasn't interested. She should have kindly shown disinterest. She should have at least given him some clue. Willow knew that if she did that Rupert would have taken it well. No hard feelings, no disrespect. That's how he was.

But instead, she followed her instinct, and she too said three little words that meant so much more than what they seemed.

"I'm so glad."

She saw the change in his face as he grinned, and that gleam returned to his eyes. Willow noted to herself how different the green was from Arthur's brown.

It was Rupert who started a proper conversation first. "So any news from Charles? I heard my mother speak to his father this morning about an arrival."

"Oh yes," Willow smiled genuinely. "He will be on the last train arriving tomorrow."

"I imagine you'll be at the station?" He led her around an old oak tree in order to make another round of the gardens.

Willow understood just hat he was doing. He was trying not to lead her too far from the general crowd. It wasn't respectable and, of course, Rupert wasn't the kind of man to place ladies in compromising positions.

"Yes, I'd love to be, but mother isn't so keen since our carriage isn't in the best shape and father's off with the motor car, you know. I'd have to walk." She sighed. It was rather disappointing that she could possibly miss her best friend's arrival back home if the weather turned out bad.

"What? All the way to the station?" Rupert was genuinely surprised, Willow thought. She also thought she felt the slightest tug on her arm to bring her closer to him. Purposefully, she edged closer to him.

"Yes, I guess."

"Nonsense, Willow, you can't do that."

"Well, I don't want to miss being there." Willow supposed he might be offering his carriage to her next and was wondering what her mother would say if she was to accept his offer.

"I'll drive you." He said simply.

"Oh," was her first reaction. It seemed to suggest that she was underwhelmed by his offer, now that she thought about it, but the case was the complete opposite. She hadn't supposed he'd offer her a ride.

"I can borrow the motor car from my father that day and we can both go to the station together." He turned to smile at her. "With your mother's permission, of course."

At this, Willow couldn't help but smile. It was this kind of thoughtfulness that she had been wanting from Arthur all along. Just a spare thought for her position and what her mother might think. But now she wondered if it really was fair to think of Arthur in this way. After all, Willow had only told him how she felt so recently, and he did promise he would be more careful from now.

Rupert sensed a change in her manner, so he added quickly, "If you're worried about a chaperone, I don't mind if you'd bring someone along. Otherwise, I think it's common around here for girls to go unchaperoned in car rides every once in a while." Then, he winked.

Willow couldn't help but blush, her cheeks started blazing and she was left no choice but to turn her head bashfully away.

She didn't like this new feeling of being so easily affected by Rupert's presence. Oh, she knew she it looked like she was flirting with him! And everyone else around her must have caught on, too. She only hoped that Arthur wouldn't get the wrong impression.

CHAPTER 21

R upert and Willow walked around together amongst the marvellous greenery and blooming flowers that made up Arthur's
family garden. It was a lovely place that made Willow feel at ease,
but it also made her feel a little tinge of guilt deep down that she
was fluttering at Rupert's presence while in Arthur's home.

They talked of general things that Willow didn't really care for
specifically, but she loved hearing the sound of his voice. That
silky-smooth baritone with its perfect inflections drove her absolutely wild and anytime his voice lowered to tell her something
particularly interesting, she felt her breath quicken and her cheeks
flush. It was all too much for her and she could hardly bring herself
to look into his eyes. But when she did- oh when she did!- it felt
like heaven. She felt like she could go on staring into his eyes for
all eternity and she'd never get tired.

The conversation somehow turned to marriage and Willow
found herself listening to Rupert's very certain proclamations that
he would remain a bachelor for the rest of his life.

"Well, you're so young, Mr Johnson, what makes you think that some pretty thing won't fall for you? I wouldn't be surprised if I see you engaged by the end of next season. Besides, if you don't mind me saying—I'm only being frank—"

"Go ahead, I don't mind frank people at all."

"You're quite agreeable to look at, in fact, I'd say you're very handsome. Now, don't tell me you haven't had any one of these girls in this part of the country not dying to be in your company? They must be. Why, I saw with my own eyes just before, Mary Caldwell must have thought something about you."

The young man shuffled his feet and smiled. "Yes, though I'm not half as rich as Arthur it'd be a lie to say I've received no attention." He paused for a while and looked about him before continuing, "You know, I'm sorry to bring up something of the kind, but despite him getting so much attention, that doesn't mean he's had an easy time. You'd be surprised how often ladies try to take advantage of Arthur's nature."

"Oh, so this has happened for sure?"

"Oh, it's happened, scores of times. The poor fellow, he takes it so unusually well. But, he happens to be different now, a little more subdued. He came to the country to settle his head a little, you see."

"Is that so?"

"Yes, apparently he had had enough of city society; what with all the balls and dinners and parties. He couldn't stand being the centre of attention all the time."

"Why, I guess nothing has changed, he's still greatly sought after."

"I know, but he thinks it to be a little better in some way. I told him to come here under another name, you know, some sort of way that he could get away from all that frivolous bustle—"

"But he wouldn't do it would he?"

"No, I couldn't even get him to think about it."

"He's so honest, is he not?"

"That's true." Rupert paused. "You haven't heard much about his society experiences, have you?"

"No, all the things I've heard about him were rumours about his father's health. Is there something you think I should know?"

"Not that you must," he was struggling to make sure he did not worry Willow, "only that you might have heard people talk of —well, of things, and people and . . . and people that he knew and the gentlemen and ladies whom—"

"Ladies, you say?" Willow's interest had been piqued, which was what Rupert was precisely trying not to do.

"Oh, only general things. If he cared too much about her, he would have been talking to everyone about—"

"Her? Who is she?" Willow checked herself, "Not that I am so greatly inclined to know."

Rupert seized his opportunity, "Well, if you do not really want to know, it isn't important at all" And with that he quickly changed the subject.

Sometime later, Arthur had finally been able to take leave of his mother, having greeted all of the guests with her. Skilfully he managed to slip by the people who were seeking to have a conversation with him, taking special care to turn down Cecilia's offers to have a tête-à-tête. Dodging people where he could and making sharp turns where possible, he made his way through the garden in search of Willow. Having reached her at Mr Johnson's side, he placed his hand gently on her waist for just a slight moment and announced his presence with a cheery, "Hello there!".

Willow and Rupert were in the middle of discussing the details for their trip to the station the next day when Willow started at the soft touch of Arthur's hand on her waist.

She turned to look at him and gave him a bright smile. Arthur was content with that; he didn't need any more from her.

"Rupert, I trust you're well?" Arthur greeted him casually.

Willow glanced over at him, "For not having seen each other in a while—"

"Oh no," Rupert interrupted, "since I've returned Arthur and I have been visiting each other."

Willow thought it was odd that Rupert hadn't mentioned that the time he came over to her house. Granted, he didn't say anything to deny having visited Arthur or spending time with him, but he just made it seem to Willow that they were not so close. All the same, she thought to herself, Arthur hadn't said anything of his friendship with Rupert. There seemed to her to be such a cloud over Arthur's past. She felt like she barely even knew him and this did not give her any reassurance in what she was doing. But, she sighed inwardly, she had already given her heart to him and it would take a great exertion to get herself over the thought of him.

"Yes," Arthur placed a hand on Rupert's shoulder and added with a laugh, "I've seen him often enough, I'm nearly bored of his face."

After a pause, Arthur continued, "Well, Willow, how are you on this frightfully mediocre day?"

"I wish you wouldn't think the day to be mediocre, I find the weather to be quite splendid, Arthur. Don't you think so too, Rupert?"

"Yes, I think it's a fine..." He didn't finish his sentence and instead turned tense.

Willow wondered what could have been wrong and she only realised when she saw Arthur turning to look behind him. There was Mary Caldwell eyeing Rupert rather obviously.

"Why, does she have no sense? Everyone can see her!" Arthur spoke softly to his two companions. He then gripped Rupert's forearm and added gently, "Though I know you don't really mind, do you? You've got a soft spot for her."

This comment was said in his usual playful manner with a tilt of the head that left his curls bouncing, but to Willow it could have been the most solemn of remarks. She took Rupert's reddening to indicate that there was indeed some inkling of feeling there, and this, for some reason unbeknownst to her, caused her breath to quicken yet again and her chest to feel heavier.

She turned to look at the girl again, who was now darting her eyes back and forth between the woman she was talking with and Rupert. She felt her cheeks reddening. Mary and Rupert, she thought to herself, what a stupid idea! Surely, Rupert was far better than her? He didn't need to stoop so low to someone as mean and plain as Mary. But here she hesitated a little, for was she not plain too in comparison to Arthur? What would others think of that? Would they be thinking what she just thought about Mary too? Her thoughts turned deeper and soon she found she had missed half of what Rupert was saying to Arthur.

"If I didn't know you so well Rupert, I'd say you're quite in love with her, good fellow."

"Well, there's nothing wrong in that. Only I don't have any money like you do." He noticed Willow's perplexed expression and took the liberty of explaining with a blush appearing on his cheeks, "N-not that I'm interested in marriage at all, or marriage to Miss Caldw—I haven't ever entertained the idea! Never, I promise. O-only that it isn't fair what certain people say about her—not that I think she's the opposite of what people say, but it just isn't right, is it?" He placed his hands firmly in his pockets, as if the whole situation was too great for his control.

Arthur moved to Willow's side and placed his arm around her waist, but Willow took hold of it and gently removed it. "He's hopelessly in love with her, you see, Willow."

"Ah, you only wish I was, and then she wouldn't be so hopelessly set on you, Arthur. Yes, that's the truth, Willow. There isn't a girl here who doesn't wish she could marry our dearest Mr Rosewood."

Just then they noticed the self same Mary walking towards them. Arthur was the first to greet her, "Why, hello Miss Caldwell, I hope you're enjoying your time?"

"Yes," she started as she straightened her rose coloured hat and looked towards Arthur, "I had hoped I would have had the opportunity to talk to you a little earlier, Mr Rosewood, I had been waiting for a chance to speak to you all this time. Then, seeing as you were busy enough with hosting, I had hoped Mr Johnson would entertain us with his company." Here she eyed him again. "But it seems he and Miss Fletcher were conversing on something evidently much more interesting than..."

Willow let out an audible sigh. She thought to herself that Mary's strategies were so very obvious and quite clearly, she was attempting to mimic Kitty.

Mary continued on for a while about how lovely the garden look and how exquisite the food was, before finally returning back to the topic of Rupert.

Arthur, clearly bored with her presence, sacrificed his friend. "Why," a smile formed on his face as if he had thought of something brilliantly clever, "Mr Johnson was just saying he wanted to see the apricot trees. How about the pair of you go together? It's wonderful in the shade out there and perhaps he could also show you my rose garden?"

Rupert reddened again and Willow felt sorry for him. He fidgeted with his sleeves and cast Arthur a cold look, which made Willow glad because it would have upset her if he had expressed any joy in spending some time, however little, with Mary alone. Why did she care at all? She wondered to herself if it was possible that it was only because she disliked Mary that she thought she held affections for Rupert, but that didn't seem like a possible explanation to her.

Reluctantly, and with a sinking feeling inside her, she watched Rupert and Mary link arms and walk off.

CHAPTER 22

Willow had tried to put away all thoughts about Rupert and Mary. There was no point in entertaining such ideas. There was no way Rupert would end up with Mary, but even if he did, it shouldn't mean anything to her. She had Arthur and she had gotten his word that he would court her the proper way, the way that he ought to court her. It is true, she did have some feelings for Rupert, whether they were romantic though was a point of contention, but she could not just do away with the fact that they were there. She went through these strange cycles of thinking him handsome one moment, and not so handsome the rest. To put it simply, she was confused. For this very reason and to ensure that her feelings did not somehow develop towards romantic inclinations, she had sent Rupert a very sweet, friendly letter to thank him for his offer of driving her to the railway station to meet her friend Charles but explain that she could not accept; her mother needed her for some errands at home and, all the same, Charles would come to call once he was settled back in the country. Rupert took it very well, as she knew he would, and sent her back a very amiable letter along with an invitation to repeat another of their walks in the park, with a chaperone, he had added.

Charles did come to the country, in good time, and brought with him some news that would keep people occupied for a good many weeks at the very least. He had been engaged in Town, not just to anyone, but to a high society socialite turned singer. A very unconventional sort of woman, of whom a few things Willow had heard being murmured in drawing rooms, but all the same, a woman who was born into a good, but moreover, wealthy family which provided her, perhaps, with a little protection.

It was on a night after a dinner hosted at Charles' parents' home, at which Willow and her mother were in attendance only, for the two families were known to dine together frequently, owing to the friendship between the two older women, that Willow had the opportunity to talk to Charles privately.

They sat on the green upholstered sofa across the room from their mothers and Willow was completely aglow, partly from the fresh breeze of the evening coming in through a window and partly from the slight overindulgence in desserts at dinner.

"Charles, you must tell me all about it," she pressed his hand in hers. "How did you ever get away with not writing me a word about all this? Why didn't you tell me a thing?"

"You must forgive me for that Willow, but I don't think I could have. It was all a condition from her mother and I wanted her so much that I would have done almost anything. You see, she's been engaged before and that did not end so well, so I think it was all to stop people from talking." Charles blushed, as he was prone to do and his loose, blonde curls were brushed decidedly away from his face, leaving his earnest and bright face clear to read. He had never quite mastered the art of concealing his feelings, so Willow could tell that he was speaking the truth.

"Never mind that now. I can't wait to meet her," Willow sighed. "She will be visiting of course?"

"Yes we are expecting her and her other quite soon. Although we will be returning to Town once the wedding is over, but that will not be for a while, Willow, and you will always be welcome to come. I think the two of you will get along famously. She's quite a charming, charming girl. So sweet and soft, I haven't met a thing as delicate as she is. Why, she's quite a pink rose."

On the day that Lady Adeline and her mother had arrived, such great commotion was stirred in the town once again. Their arrival by automobile only added to this confused chatter and excitement. Whilst Lady Adeline's mother, the Lady de Brackett, was found to be quite a confirmed socialite within the first week of their arrival, no one in the town had been in the presence of the singer. Whenever Lady de Brackett received home visits, her daughter would never make an appearance, apparently being too tired from the journey, save for when Charles paid visits to her. According to him and Lady de Brackett, the match was perfect; it was of great relief to Lady Adeline's mother that Mr Charles Daniels, Esquire had indeed a relatively extensive amount of wealth in property and investments. Naturally, the pair was the constant obsession of all home visit conversations and the subject of fixation of the young ladies. Willow had lost her hopes of meeting Charles' fiancée any time soon, concluding that the singer probably despised country company. Thus, the invitation which she received by calling card from Lady de Brackett seemed so out of place. Strangely, the invitation was only directed towards Willow, for Lady Adeline especially wanted to have a small meeting with Charles and Willow alone. Not wanting the opportunity to pass, Willow soon wrote that she was to be expected for the next day at lunchtime.

Having arrived at the country house, which was rented out by the mother and daughter for their holiday, Willow was not surprised to find that Charles had arrived before her, and that Lady de Brackett was nowhere to be seen. As she entered the drawing room, behind the maid that was announcing her, Willow caught her breath. Lady Adeline was truly a sight to behold; perhaps it was not all due to natural appearance, more likely to her fine dress and toilette, but Willow was amazed all the same. The lady seemed to be a year or two older than Willow and about the same age as Charles, although she did not look any taller than her. Lady Adeline's fine brown ringlets were placed so as to frame her rosy face perfectly, a face that Willow was sure never braved the sun bare without shade. Her pastel pink day dress, with all its rose and flower embellishments, lay spread out around her as she was stretched out on the long divan. Charles was seated on a chair at the head of the divan, leaning in closely and talking softly into her ear. From where she was standing at the door, Willow could hear her friend's soft mutterings and Lady Adeline's silvery laughter and her perfectly inflected tones. In comparison, Willow was sure that Kitty seemed insignificant.

The heads of Charles and Lady Adeline turned towards the door, as Willow was announced and she walked in. Her hostess exerted no efforts to stand, but rather opted to hold herself up on her lithe arm and smile beamingly up at Willow, as Charles stood to greet his friend.

"It is an absolute pleasure to meet you, Miss Phillips," Lady Adeline began after she pointed an armchair by her divan to Willow.

"Please, call me Willow, Lady Adeline." She was beginning to feel that Adeline was an amicable lady.

"Well, you must call me Adeline then. Tell me, do you want cake or biscuits with your tea?" She asked with such niceness that Willow was decided that she positively liked her altogether, but she was unable to put a finger on where that niceness derived.

The maid that Lady Adeline was giving orders to for the tea was awaiting Willow's response. Promptly, she replied, "Cake, please."

"Why," Lady Adeline beamed with such delight, "cake is also my favourite. I have a feeling that we will be best of friends. I am in dire need of company here in the country."

"I too, Adeline, think that we will be such great friends. And I never make such claims."

"That's true, dear," Charles felt it necessary to support Willow's claim, "Willow isn't one to make false claims."

"That's all the better, for I like to think myself to be the very same."

"That's also true, dear," and he took her hand and pressed it to his lips.

"I adore you so dearly, Charlie."

"I only more, my own," He added as he pressed her hand to his chest.

Willow, despite liking these two people, found the whole scene simply pathetic, and, for the want of another subject to rest her eyes on, began to study the furnishings in the room. They were very elaborate and not what the previous tenant would have left. Thus, she was able to conclude that Lady de Brackett and her daughter would have been well aware of their coming long before Charles' last correspondence to Willow. In fact, Charles would have known of the whole ordeal, weeks prior, but never did he tell Willow a word of any engagement to any young lady. Willow did not expect him to reveal the identity of his fiancée at any previous time, for it certainly would have caused her to be under pressure from everyone else in the small town, but she would have liked to have known that an engagement had taken place. Then, she thought, she would have been less worried about the situation between him and Kitty.

Willow turned back to the conversation in front of her, although she was fairly ignored by the two; they only went so far as to restrict their displays for the knowledge of the presence of a close friend.

"And when does the Lady de Brackett return, my sweet?"

"I don't expect Mama to arrive at any time before lunchtime is quite over. Won't you stay a little longer, dear?"

"I do not think I will be able to; I have some things to attend to, I've been away for so long. But I will leave you here with Willow, you will not be alone." He kissed her hand once again and stood up.

She stood up after him and said to Willow smilingly, "I will follow Charlie to the door. I apologise for leaving you, but I will be back shortly."

"Goodbye, Willow." Charles said, rather weakly she thought.

Willow expressed that it was no matter, said her goodbyes to Charles and watched the couple walk out of the drawing room hand in hand whilst Lady Adeline rested her head on Charles' shoulder.

In the short time spent alone, Willow began to ponder how pleasant it would be if Arthur made up his mind at any time and decided whether he did or, in fact, did not want to marry Willow. For she felt so much in the dark when it came to his true affections, that she did not know how to speak about him to others. She had made up her mind, for the time being, not to mention him in front of Lady Adeline. To Willow, the singer seemed like the sentimental kind, who would be certain to make assumptions out of things, so it would have been safer not to mention Arthur at all.

Shortly, Lady Adeline returned, and thrust herself listlessly onto the divan, sending her skirts aflutter. Willow thought she looked like a personified butterfly.

"I have the fullest belief," Adeline began, leaning in towards Willow, "that we shall be like sisters."

"I would like that, for I have no sisters or close female companions of my own."

"We are so alike, Willow, for I find myself to be in the same situation."

"No, you, with such fame. You must be delighted within the best circles of society."

"It is true," she said with a melancholic tone, that Willow was inclined to find rather too dramatic for her tastes.

A pause ensued until she spoke again, "It is true. I am admired by all and loved by none, except for my darling Charlie, you see. All ladies are quite jealous of me."

"Certainly not all?"

"Those that aren't married, of course."

"Why, I could admire you Adeline, but I would not be jealous—"

"Oh, but not you," Adeline sighed with childish annoyance as she knotted her eyebrows. "You have a beau."

"What makes you think so?"

"By the way you talk; you're confident enough to let me know that you have found someone that cares for you."

"Are you really inclined to believe so?"

"Quite and I'm never wrong; I have experience in this."

"Well," Willow hesitated, "you might be right."

"Aren't you sure he returns your affections?"

"Oh, he returns them well over, but—"

"But will he marry you?" Lady Adeline leaned forward again, but this time with a flash of excitement across her eyes.

CHAPTER 23

Willow couldn't help but feel just a little unease in that room now. Lady Adeline's sparkling eyes now seemed to make her appear almost cat-like in nature.

"I can only hope for the best of you, Willow. But, hear me, if he does not marry you, he must be a fool, for you strike me as a very sensible girl." She took a bite out of her cake.

Willow shuffled in her seat.

As though nothing had occurred, Lady Adeline continued, "What is there to do here that requires little mingling with people?"

Willow thought. "Walking in the park is quite pleasant."

"Walk?" Lady Adeline began to laugh. "Let me tell you one thing: I do not take walks in parks. Not because I think myself to be above it, but because I cannot stand the people I meet." She paused to think. "How about riding? Yes, riding shall do. I might ride about every now and then."

"I am sorry that you do not like walking because I find it to be most helpful, especially when there is something to think about."

"That is how you met him then?"

"Met who?" Willow pretended not to know.

"Why, him!" Lady Adeline pushed herself back into the divan. "It is, isn't it?"

"Perhaps, Adeline," Willow did not want to risk drawing Adeline's attention to Arthur, for she thought, jealously, that he might be tempted by her beauty, "and perhaps not. I shall tell you about it another time."

"Very well, but I am sure to know about it soon enough." She shifted restlessly in her seat, "Let me tell you something about Charles; I find him to be so kind and gentle, I've never been treated with such sincerity of devotion before."

"I hope," Willow checked herself from making too offensive a statement, "well, I know, that you shall not be like those girls who try to take advantage of his inclination to devotion."

"Certainly not, Willow. Not at all. You don't know me well enough yet, I suppose."

She rang the bell that she had in one of her pockets. "Susan, bring the sandwiches please." She turned to Willow after taking a couple herself, "Now, help yourself, dear."

Willow took a sandwich. "Won't Lady de Brackett be joining us?"

"Dear no! Would Lady de Brackett want to have lunch in such a casual manner? No, she makes every daily event a social event. Well, she's out now at the moment having lunch with some Robert-sons or Richards."

"Is that so?"

"Mother tells me their daughter, Catherine I believe, is quite keen to be married into wealthy society and says I should be quite lucky I did not lose Charles."

"I can also support that, Catherine Richards, is in every essence seeking to be married into that kind of society. I know her personally."

"Well, is she pretty?"

Usually, Willow would have answered 'yes' only, but Lady Adeline was so exceptionally beautiful that Willow felt herself compelled to use her face as the standard. "She isn't plain, but not an exceptionally beauty. She is pretty."

"Ah, she's a snob, I believe? People like her are always snobs."

"Yes, you could call her that." Willow replied seriously.

Lady Adeline sighed, paused, and changed the subject. "I hear we are not the only ones come from town recently. Apparently Mr Arthur Rosewood, Lord Rosewood's son, and Mr Rupert Johnson, more recently, are here too?"

Willow tried not to reveal her despair at finding out that Adeline did in fact know Arthur. "That is correct."

"Would I also be correct in saying that one of the two gentlemen in question is your beau? Namely, Mr Rosewood?" Lady Adeline smiled, rather sweetly with her green eyes sparkling.

Willow did not reply.

"Come, you may tell me," she took Willow's hand in hers.

From her silence, Lady Adeline assumed herself, "Oh, it is true then!" And she leaped up with such joy and energy that astounded Willow. She embraced her tightly and made Willow take a seat by her on the divan.

"I am assuming you know Mr Rosewood personally then, Adeline? May I ask how you are connected to him?"

"Oh, my mother, being the socialite she is, knows Lord Rosewood quite well. And I, despite my beauty and talent, have never really had the opportunity (or the success, if I confess) to woo his son Mr Rosewood at all. In fact, I think I am making an understatement if I were to describe his sentiment towards me as a disdain."

Lady Adeline spoke with this with a touch of embarrassment, but held her head high as she proclaimed, rather vengefully Willow thought, "Although, he is quite penniless now. But don't tell anyone, I only feel it is my duty to tell you. Mother says Lord Rosewood blew quite nearly the whole fortune away on his special medications for his perfectly fine health." She lowered her tone, "There is talk that he is, well let's just say, slightly hypochondriac tendencies"

As Willow saw it, especially through Lady Adeline's detailed explanation of Arthur's fall from title of a lord's son to poor gentility, the girl did not seem to have any trace of any incentive to go after Arthur. Arthur was, as Lady Adeline thought, a hopeless cause. And she said, "His good looks will get him nowhere in life."

Willow was quite ready to become severely offended on behalf of Arthur for all of these statements, until Lady Adeline realised. "Oh, but I do not mean it to offend. I am sure that he loves you very much, for you seem like the kind of simple girl that Mama thought Mr Rosewood would prefer over the seasoned society belles. And if he loves you, my dear, then nothing else matters, does it? Why, I would marry Charles all the same even if he did not have a cent to his name!" And she began laughing aloud in her melodious tones once again.

Despite not being badly humoured at all, Willow thought that Lady Adeline was indeed lying.

Time passed on and soon it was time for Willow to leave and she left, feeling that she had truly gained a friend, despite however much money-centred she may seem.

On her walk to the general market, straight after the visit, Willow was spotted by Arthur who came running to her, generally curious to hear about the event. She contemplated coming up with an excuse to leave straight away, but thought better of it.

"Good morning, dear. How are you?" Arthur asked, as he comfortably placed his arm across her shoulders.

Granted, they were in the middle of practically nowhere and no one would be walking down that road at this time, but Willow was still a little irritated by this, especially since she was just recently thinking of his intentions and of whether he would ever marry her. "I am fine," she replied curtly.

"I am good too. In fact—"

"I never asked you, Arthur, but I am sure that you are alright." She kept walking, trying to act as indifferent as possible.

"Say, what did that Lady Adeline fill your head with?" He was growing concerned, and Willow was aware of this.

"Nothing that should worry you at all."

"You saying that does quite the opposite," he held her arm firmly, but not painfully. "Will you please tell me?" She looked into his brown eyes, and Willow already knew that her self-restraint would come undone. There they were, those stunning, glistening brown eyes.

She leaned in closer to him and whispered, "Only that she once tried to get your attention and you, at least, disdain her altogether."

"So why must you be—"

"And that you are penniless."

He paused, rather startled, Willow thought. He didn't talk for a few seconds and then started laughing. "Is that what concerns you? That I'm poor. Do you think that if you were to marry me then—"

He stopped himself at that point and placed both his hands in his pockets.

"Do go on," Willow turned to him with open eyes and Arthur was struck by her earnestness.

"W-well, do you think that I would let you marry me while I am poor and cannot provide for you? Don't you think that I would at least try, to my full capabilities, to acquire some sort of wealth before I would propose to you?"

Willow turned back to face the road ahead of her, "My doubts lie not on whether you will be preoccupied with how to provide for me, but if you are intending on marrying me at all."

There, she had said it, and it was a great relief. Swiftly, she brought out her handkerchief to wipe her moist eyes, but she cursed herself for it, since she thought it only made her look weaker in front of him.

With his usually gleefulness, he began, as if he expected this question to come, "And what would lead you to believe that I want to marry in general? Not just you, but anybody. Oh, is that what concerns you so much? Well, perhaps you should have paid a little closer attention to the changes that you've caused in me, darling. Why, I believe I'm quite the marrying kind now. Only," he smiled to himself, "I have no money, as Lady Adeline says."

"So, you would marry me, would you?" She stopped walking and embraced him tightly. He kissed both her hands repeatedly, until she asked again, "Oh, so you would?"

"Most certainly, my dear, sweet Willow! Is that even a question I must ask myself?"

"Even if I have no money of my own. Since you're quite poor yourself and I've nothing to give, you could have quite married someone rich to save yourself."

"Who says that Lady Adeline is right anyway?" He laughed softly at her perplexed face. "No, she lies to you or at least not willingly, for there are many stories about my father. Promise me not to believe a word she says; she's rather dramatic. I've got just the same fortune as I had always, nothing has changed."

"Why, that's—that's great, Arthur." She checked around for any onlookers.

"Were you going to the market? Let's not go. Come, I'd rather spend some time under the trees."

So they made their way to a shady, secluded area of the park and sat themselves cosily on the foot of the tree. Arthur, having set down his hat and Willow's straw hat before them, pulled Willow closer to him. He kissed her cheeks alternatively and, between giving and taking kisses, told her, "I'm so glad I came to the country or else I would have never met you."

"I'm awfully glad too, Arthur, and I still can't believe that it is all quite true. You seem like a dream to me."

She let her eyes wonder over his green vest and smiled, happily. He brought her even closer again and Willow rested her head on his chest, passively rising and falling as he breathed.

"You love me Willow?"

She nodded.

"But why? Aren't I just a city dandy?"

"No you're not. There's nothing more wonderful than you. But you love me Arthur, why?"

"How could I not? You are simply everything that I had longed for, so level-headed and sensible, why, I could never do any wrong under your guidance."

"That is to say, you'll marry me?" She looked at him.

"I would certainly like to."

"Why, then propose." She sat up and fixed her hair.

"Is it necessary? We both know—"

"Absolutely necessary. Now, kneel down and go ahead."

He followed the directions. "Will you marry me, my darling Willow?"

"Oh, I will, Arthur."

CHAPTER 24

The news of the engagement soon spread around and Willow and Arthur's wedding was scheduled to take after Charles and Lady Adeline's wedding. Kitty paid some very bitter congratulations to Arthur and rather cordial ones to Willow. In all, the two were content that they could at least display their affection more openly in public. One afternoon, Willow went to visit Lady Adeline, as this became a daily routine for her to visit the secluded city girl. However, she always tried to keep Arthur's warning at hand, so she never completely believed the stories she was told.

She entered her chambers and found Lady Adeline swooping on her sofa.

"Ah, Willow, congratulations with the engagement; it is most wonderful news!" She bid Willow to come closer so she could plant a kiss on her cheek.

"Thank you, Adeline."

"How changed you are! Your cheeks are twice as rosy as they usually are." She sighed. "I remember when I changed in that way."

"When Charles proposed?" She took a seat.

"Goodness, no. Charles' proposal was rather expected and commonplace."

"Why, have you been engaged before?"

Lady Adeline looked at Willow and a cunning smile passed her lips for a moment before the usual placid smile took its place. "Many times. They never worked. Especially the last one."

"And to who were you engaged to?"

"Oh, mon dieu! You wouldn't believe me if I told you." She put on one of her melancholic airs and raised her pale arm to her forehead. "You would think me an invalid of sorts."

"No, Adeline, do tell me."

"If you insist," she did not need much coaxing to get the matter out of her, "well, there was dear Robert, then Francis and Oliver—"

"I'm sorry, Adeline, but I do not any of them."

"There is someone you will know," she paused. "The latest engagement that had been broken off. It was Mr Rosewood."

Willow froze. She felt the heat rise to her cheeks. It just absolutely could not be. She despised the whole room altogether. Why had she ever started a friendship with this woman? How dare she talk to her in such a way about her own fiancee? Was this some kind of joke to her? It was not just to make such accusations about people's fiancees.

"Yes, I knew you would react in that way." Lady Adeline got up from the sofa, moving languidly towards the dressing table. To Willow, this was the ultimate betrayal, knowing about it all along, but never telling her until now. And still! Lady Adeline made no fuss about it, as if it was a casual matter. But could she believe what she was saying or was this only to rouse her jealousy?

Willow still did not know what to say.

She laughed, "You don't believe me do you?"

"It is no laughing matter. If this is a farce, come out with it, for I do not appreciate it."

Instead of replying, Lady Adeline opened a drawer, took out a key and used it to open another drawer. From the locked drawer, she took out a small pocket book and a box. Bringing the objects towards Willow she said, "Here. You cannot assume everyone to be an absolute angel like you, Willow. And you should not be so trusting as well."

Willow opened the box and found it was packed with rose perfumed letters that were bearing Arthur's bold, cursive hand. She picked one out and scanned random lines, My dearest, my one and only eternal desire, I find that my love for you grows only deeper each second I spend in your presence … She stopped reading, it was unbearable. Next, she opened the pocket book, and one of Arthur's curly brown locks fell out. By now, Willow was burning with rage. She had managed to hold back her tears, for Lady Adeline's presence behind her fuelled her hatred so much as to dry her moist eyes. Willow did not need to look at many pages of the pocket book to realise it was a journal kept by Lady Adeline during the time before she was engaged to Arthur. She put the objects back into their positions and handed them to Lady Adeline.

"Now you believe me? Arthur never spoke a word about this, did he? Such a shame too, for it was not too long ago." She returned the objects to their drawer and locked it.

"Do you still love him?"

"Me? No, the question is whether he still loves me. And I am sure he does. How could he not?"

Willow found herself saying aloud, "Indeed."

Lady Adeline returned to her sofa and hid her face behind her hands. She was smiling like a child behind her hands, which Willow found curiously strange.

"I believed you when you said he was penniless and you did not want him—"

"That was a lie, darling."

"Then, why—"

"It wasn't me." Lady Adeline laughed again. "I wouldn't be marrying Charles, I would be having another try with Arthur. He refused me. How could he? I know. That is what I am still thinking. The fool, he said he cared for me and loved me and adored me, but he still decided to leave me!" She pouted childishly, "It'll be his loss anyway. Well, he's got you now."

"And why did you pretend to be my friend?"

"Well, I had to keep an eye on how Arthur was and what he was up to. I just had to know whether he had a change of heart. I've had private conversations with him—"

Willow started, "What?"

She continued as if nothing had happened, "—and he told me how much he still cared for me, but that he had found you et cetera. He's a fool for not wanting me back. Besides, I still liked you since you were so lovely, but I still managed to teach you that not everyone is honest."

"Have you told Charles?"

"Did Arthur tell you?" Willow was silent. "Exactly."

"What stops me from telling Charles?"

Lady Adeline smiled mischievously, the corners of her mouth curling, "What stops me from tempting Arthur? I've done it before;

made plenty of young gentlemen like him do things for me, I could do it again."

"You're detestable." Willow stood up, clenching her fists and stomping her foot.

"You'd better be careful, huh?" She opened up her fan and began fanning herself. "Well, I'll see you at the wedding; I don't suppose you will be coming back again."

"I certainly won't."

"Good riddance, Willow. I wish you a wonderful day and a blessed marriage."

Willow stormed off at the sound of that harmonic, silvery laughter.

"What a whole lot of explaining Arthur has to do," Willow thought to herself, "and did he think he could make a fool out of him? Well, he'll have to answer to me first. How dare he keep the truth away from me? Does he think me stupid?" And so she continued, right up until she reached Mr Rosewood's home.

Once she reached his home, the butler insisted on her coming back another time as Mr Rosewood was not prepared to take in guests or that she should kindly leave a calling card. Trying to communicate the urgency of the situation, Willow asked him to announce her to Mr Rosewood. So, the butler went and then returned with the notice that Mr Rosewood would kindly be ready to receive his guest in ten minutes' time. This only infuriated Willow and she decidedly walked past the butler, out of the drawing room, and into the study that she saw him enter before. Despite the butler's calls to be a little more patient, Willow opened the doors on her own and entered the room.

Arthur was standing by a cabinet, fixing his hair in the looking-glass and adjusting his shirt sleeves. To see him making sure that he was well-dressed for her, on any other day, would have made Willow overjoyed that he cared about the impression he made on her. However, today, it only made Willow more impatient and angry; to think that he never really cared for her and it was all in order to forget Lady Adeline.

He was surprised when he heard her take a few steps towards an armchair. He turned around and his face lit up with joy, "Ah, Willow, you couldn't wait, could you? Well, neither could I, but I was just fixing up my—"

"Spare me from listening to your vain ramblings, Arthur." She felt a little out of breath and had to lean her arm on the head of the chair.

"What do you mean?"

"What do I mean, indeed, Arthur? For I have just heard of some news that you were previously engaged."

He walked towards her, but she moved behind the armchair for a barrier. "That might be true; in fact, it is true. Is there any wrong in having been engaged in the past?"

"Don't you think you would have told me?"

"Well, I have. Didn't I tell you of all the high society I used to mingle with and the conceited ladies I was forced to dance with?"

"Yes, you did. But you never spoke of engagements."

"Wouldn't you think it only natural that being surrounded with such beautiful, eligible young women would lead me to becoming engaged at least once?"

That was true; Willow did have some knowledge of a possibility of him being engaged prior. "I always assumed they were not very serious relationships or courtships, whatever you might want to call them."

"You assumed correctly." He tried to move closer.

Willow, moving to the other side of the armchair, said, "But, dear Arthur," she paused as she delighted at the effect that her sarcastic tone had on him, "I have heard that this particular engagement was quite serious, especially on your part."

He sighed. "That might be, but I wish you'd come out with it already. Who told you this? And what engagement are you speaking about?"

"Oh, so there have been numerous ones; too many to know which one I talk of?"

"Not so many," he ran his hand through his hair, and spoiled the curls he had been ordering so carefully before, "There has been just one."

"Why, just one!" She continued her sarcasm. "Now, wouldn't it have been so simple for you to tell me about it? Well, even to hint at whom it might have involved. What if I were to find out?"

"You would have come to me, I figured; just as you are now." He smiled cunningly.

Willow could not let him have any pleasure in her jealousy. "Is that so? Therefore, I've found it out, you think. Because I have nothing better to do, but go around making inquiries about you in general and collecting information from different unreliable sources and basing my image of you on mere gossip? Well, I don't think I would have liked you to tell me about yourself a little more, directly. No, that would not do, never. Why would Willow want that? You thought, Oh, I'll just let her do her usual country snooping about and finding things out about me. Eventually, she'll come to know about it, hey? And she'll confront me and then I'll just be a little evasive and console her, like a little child, and she'll be back to her simple-minded loving state. Now, don't say that's what you didn't think Arthur." She ended by decidedly crossing her arms over her chest as she said the last sentence.

"How can I say it isn't what I thought, when it obviously was?"

"I don't believe a word, Arthur."

"Let me know how much you know." He grew confused at his own words. "Please, tell me what you know."

"I have just come directly from Lady Adeline's—"

"So you've heard it from her directly," he threw himself savagely into the armchair and made Willow jump back.

"Yes, I ought to have heard it from one of you. Why does it affect you so much?"

"Only that I know what a mess of things she's made. You see, she told me, when I broke the engagement, that if she'd ever meet another girl that I'd engaged, she would ruin it all for me and tell her what an injustice it had been."

"Well, she knew you wouldn't do it yourself, so she's right in that." Willow walked over and took a seat in the chair beside him.

"Don't justify her actions; you don't know her as I do. If you did, you wouldn't be accusing me in such a way. She isn't even half as decent as you think her to be—"

"More on her character later, Arthur. Now, you listen to me." And her face grew hot from his lack of eye contact with her and his overall gloomy state. She thought, How dare he act like the victim in this situation; what could have Lady Adeline possibly done to upset him? "I've come from Lady Adeline's and she has been so kind as to tell me of your relation to each other and show me a few memorabilia from the time. Don't you think, Arthur, that you could have told me some time? Or were you planning on not telling me at all?"

He took a few seconds to compose himself and sit upright in the armchair, "I don't know how to tell you at all, Willow. If you go on accusing me in such a way." Arthur stood up from his seat and paced about the room, "Y-you see the whole thing . . . . W-well, I-I haven't quite the damned idea where to start—"

"You could start by using some proper language," she retorted.

"Proper language!" He turned his back to her and laughed help-lessly, she had never heard him laugh in that way. "How can I even begin to tell you of the whole thing with proper language? The whole thing's a damned nonsense! That's what it is." And he laughed again, as he paced the room even faster.

"Well, if you aren't prepared to tell me—"

"No, I'm not at all."

"—I will just leave then." She stoop up, neared the door and expecting him to come up to her; she hesitated, but he never moved.

He stood at the one spot, "Well, leave then, Willow. Come again another day and I'll tell you all about it when I'm more composed."

"You think I'll be waiting for you?" She laughed amidst tears that were forming in her eyes. "Oh, dear, no! I'll be gone, Mr Rosewood, and you can quite forget about me."

Arthur looked up from the carpet he was staring at, surprised at her calling him 'Mr Rosewood'. However, before he could near her to apologise, she had quit the room and shut the door with a decided bang.

Walking towards his desk, Arthur picked up a pen and began writing a note to Rupert, which he asked the butler to make sure that it was delivered to his house as quickly as possible by one of the footmen.

CHAPTER 25

The next morning, not receiving a reply from his friend, Arthur was coordinating all of the servants to finalise the packing of his luggage. He stated that important business called him to return to the city and that he would probably be engaged for some while in town. As he was sitting at his desk, packing useless papers and stationary to occupy his time, Rupert dashed in unannounced into the room. His hair was disorderly, his tennis clothes rummaged and it seemed as though he had been running.

"Arty, what's the matter?" He came to halted stop at the desk and leant with both his arms on it.

"Well, it's high time you came. I've been expecting you since yesterday."

"I know, I'm awfully sorry; that devilishly incorrigible new foot-man of mine failed to give me your note. And your telephone calls were unanswered for I was out the whole day. I was playing tennis with Cousin Cecilia and her lot this morning when the footman finally decided to man up and tell me he had forgotten the note."

"It's no matter now, I'm off."

"Yes, I've realised from the packing, the servants told me you were off to the city; is it true?"

He nodded. "I have no reason to remain."

"But Willow—"

'Don't speak of her, she's quite gone—"

Rupert gasped, "You don't mean Lady Adeline—"

"Quite."

"Well, I always told you that she was trouble, I could tell from her lazy disposition. Lazy people are always to be dealt with caution, I say."

Arthur got up from his seat and began wandering about the room.

"Did you try explaining to her?"

"I couldn't."

"What do you mean you couldn't?" Rupert ran up to him and seized him by his shoulders.

Arthur shrugged, "It wouldn't come out. I told her to come the next day, but she told me she'll never see me again."

"Confound it all! Of course, she wouldn't want to see you again, after what Lady Adeline told her. Why, I wouldn't come back to you if Adeline told me that story."

"She said she saw proof; memorabilia or something of the sort, she was saying."

"You used to write her sheets and sheets more than once a day! You don't think she would have kept some of those? Well, I don't like being mean to you, but you've been infinitely stupid, Arty."

He shook Rupert's hands off his shoulders. "Right, that is why I am leaving."

"What did you call me for yesterday then if you've already given up, you lazy sloth?" He tried to cheer him up through humour, but Arthur merely smiled a listless smile and his face moulded back into a firm line.

"I thought that you might have been able to explain things to her, but it's too late now, Rupert."

He stood thinking. "It just isn't, you know."

"She would have already told that Charles of hers and then I would be totally out of the question; they seem quite well together, I think Lady Adeline and I would be cast out."

"No," Rupert was in thoughtful meditation, "she cares for him far too much, in a friendly way, you see, to tell him the truth about his fiancée. I think I might have a chance at sorting out this mess of yours you know."

"Would you?" Arthur's face brightened.

"I've helped you before—"

"Tonnes of times, old boy."

"—I just could do it again?"

"You could, Rupert."

"And now I'll be off, Arty." And he dashed out of the room as unexpectedly as he had entered it.

Finding Willow was not so much of a hard task as Rupert thought that it was going to be. Not finding her in the park, he rushed to her home and asked her mother to speak to her. Willow's mother went up to her daughter's room to inform her daughter of the young gentleman that was wishing to speak to her.

Willow interrupted before her mother could finish, "It isn't Arthur, is it? If it is, you ought to send him back."

"No, Willow, it isn't. It's Mr Johnson, he wants to speak with you."

"And why should I speak with him, mother?" She picked up some papers she had been writing, "I've just written Arthur a very angry letter, you see. In such a heated tone that I think I have virtually washed myself of all anger towards him; I am quite cool now."

"Mr Johnson does seem very eager to speak to you. Besides, he might have some information; you know that I don't completely believe that story Lady Adeline told you. From what I have gathered from being acquainted with the Lady de Brackett, they are quite a tale-telling duo; I wouldn't believe a word she says." She paused. "But the letters and locks of hair you speak of, maybe Mr Johnson could assist with. Won't you come and speak to him? It would be so rude to send him back; and I find him to be such an agreeable fellow."

"Alright then," Willow folded the letter and slipped it into her pocket. "I'll see him."

"Do fix your hair then," her mother said as she quitted the room.

With a vain attempt at fixing her hair once or twice, Willow rushed out of her room and hurried down the stairs as she would usually on any other perfectly normal day, which only worked to disorder her hair more than before. Upon reaching the drawing room, she drew on a face of collected coolness.

"How are you Mr Johnson?" She shook his outstretched hand and took a place opposite of him and beside her mother on the sofa.

"Quite fine," was his half-mumbled reply as he sat down. "I think you know what I have come here for—"

"To tell us of your esteemed friend's good character, I presume." Willow said without looking in his direction."

"The opposite, in face. To reveal some truths and explain what I can of his path, which he could not himself."

"It seems to me not that he's perfectly incapable of recounting events that took place not too long ago, but that he does not want to."

Willow's mother interrupted, "Won't you please listen to Mr Johnson without retorting, Willow? I am sure he will be of some assistance. Do go on, Mr Johnson."

"Thank you, Mrs Phillips. What caused my friend's in-capabilities does not matter at this present moment, but I can tell you that it is because he was troubled in damaging your image of him. What I would like to tell you firstly is of how highly Arthur esteems and adores you. Honestly—"

"I am sorry to interrupt Mr Johnson," Willow's mother began, "but I think I ought to leave at this point. I trust that you and Willow will be fine," she stood up as he nodded, "If I am needed, ask the maid to call for me." And she quitted the room, in the hopes that Rupert's speech might have more effect on her daughter if they were left alone.

"Before you resume, Rupert," Willow said as she took the letter out of her pocket, "I would like you to read this letter I have addressed to Arthur." She held it out to him.

After browsing through a few lines, he said, "Well, you are justifiably angry."

"Of course. Now, all of those things, no matter how bitter or cruel they are, I would like to say to Arthur in person."

Rupert smiled.

"What is it?"

"You wouldn't be able to, for he is returning to the city today."

Willow stood up abruptly. "Today, is he?"

He nodded.

"And why does he think he may leave me?"

"He can't stand to know that you detest him and he would rather banish himself back to his monotonous society life rather than be vexing you."

"I didn't expect him to leave," she said more to herself than to Rupert.

"Neither did I, but he is quite hurt."

"What for? Why does he think he is the victim in this?" She crossed her arms.

"You don't know the story half as much as you think you do."

"So you say—'

"And you never gave him the chance to explain himself yesterday without pressuring him. He's quite given up on winning you back."

"And where can I learn this story from then?"

"Certainly not from him," he laughed softly, "that's why I'm here. And I'll be able to tell it much better than him; not biased at all, I'll be able to show you just how wicked Lady Adeline was and just how stupid your dear Arty was."

"HE isn't stupid, don't justify his—"

"Oh, he was, indeed." Rupert stretched himself out on the sofa, "Quite foolish. I tried telling him, but he never listened."

Willow took her seat again, "So, Lady Adeline was fond of him?"

"More fond of his fat wallet than him, as anybody would tell you. She was the belle of society in that year—this is three years ago I speak of—she was incomparable. Arty was serious about marriage then, for some reason, and he thought it was high time he should be treating the society season seriously (as no rich young man ever does, only poor ones like me take it seriously). Well, he cast off each young lady as being too materialistic or interested in his money and name rather than him (which were all true, by the way), and was on the verge on giving up, when he and I met Lady Adeline at some earl's dinner party. She was the guest of honour, escorted by her mother, and she was featured by being asked to sing some sentimental light opera aria about romance or something other. Having figured out who Mr Rosewood was, by her usual snooping about and sticking her wobbly nose into everyone's conversations, her mother had gotten him to sing up there. I trust you know how well Arty can sing?"

Willow nodded, smiling a little, "Perfectly angelic."

"Well," Rupert smiled to himself, "I think it a pathetically senti-mental quality, but some quite like it. So they sang and whatnot. Now, Lady Adeline with her coquettish smiles and airs and sighs and looks had, by staying with Arty and I so often, won over both of our affections. I recall very clearly, though Arthur denies it, that she had us battling each other for her attention, for we were both so desperate to win her undying attention and claim her as our own. Well, she was after Arty's money after all, so I may say I was lucky. With false promises of devotion and loyalty, Adeline had won his affection. In public, it was very well known that they had affections for each other and an engagement was expected. Arthur did all that materialistic, sentimental, romantic rubbish that he and I always despised, and sent her letters and letters a day and locks of his hair and jewellery and flowers. Gee, the flowers, Miss Phillips, you would not believe it! Things went on in this manner, for a whole year—now, this was indeed a very long time. Arthur was always asking for them to be engaged, but Adeline always put him off it in one way or another. They were secretly engaged about four or five times, and she had broken it off each time, telling him that she was interested in another and now engaged to someone else. She tormented him in such a way because she knew that he would never leave her. It pleased Adeline to expose his misery to the public and be able to claim it as a result of her winning over his heart. Despite me telling him to leave her at once, Arty continued on with Adeline, hoping that he might show her the right path." He paused to see Willow's expression, and was content at seeing her lips form into a sad form. "He simply would not listen to anybody's other opinion of Adeline; to him she was perfect. Finally, Adeline had finished her fun flirting with far poorer gentlemen, and turned her mind back to business, with much coaxing from her mother, and the two were formally engaged. A few weeks before the wedding, however, it was found out that Adeline had a secret—er, how would I say it—well, a lover of some sorts and, as you can imagine, this shook Arthur completely. It was the last straw (though I knew that if he wasn't so stupid—"

"But he wasn't stupid, Mr Johnson, he was only being his kind, affectionate self!" Willow's voice quivered slightly and she coughed, trying to compose herself. "He couldn't help it; it was all Lady Adeline's doing. Now, please, don't call him stupid again."

"Surely," Rupert apologised. "It was the last straw, even for the affectionate Arthur. He broke off the engagement and never really appeared in society that often and, when he did, he could not stand Adeline's nerve; for she did not cease and still continued pursuing him. He continued being cold towards her (though if I were him I would be a little more than cold). She made such a public display of her grief over being shunned by her former fiancée at her desperately melodramatic life story, that she had somehow won the pity of the old ladies and young ladies and stout ladies and thin ladies alike of strange city society. She never really got over it and some weeks later she managed to find Arty and I alone at a party and told him that she would never cease trying to win him back because she was 'well accustomed to Arthur's weak and sentimental disposition'. When I, angry as I was, found it within me to speak to her without hitting her head (I dare say to you Miss Phillips, don't tell Cousin Cecilia I ever thought of hitting a lady), I asked her of what she could do when Arty was married and matters were out of her control. Well, she answered that she would find out whoever he was engaged too and present his love for her so untruthfully as to make any young woman infuriatingly jealous. We were both left holding each other back so as not to take our rage out on her and she never communicated a word to us since then. Not even since she has arrive here; she has probably told you she has spoken to him, but wouldn't be true at all."

Willow had to take a full three minutes' time to recover from the effect of the story. She stood up, walked about the drawing room, went to the tea table, sipped some tea, returned to the sofa, and threw herself down. Presently, she took out her handkerchief and cried into it. Rupert stood up and went over to comfort her, "You did not know, Miss Phillips."

"Well, I've been so cruel to him." She cried some more, then wiped her eyes. "I strongly dislike criers, Mr Johnson. What do you think I should do now? Oh, you've been so useful to Arthur and I, you're such a great friend. Tell me what to do about Charles. I never told him for I was under the impression Lady Adeline had told him—and to think, I had been avoiding him and being curt; I thought that he too had been hiding Arthur's actions from me."

"I think you ought to tell Charles—you and Arthur, that is—and Lady Adeline will take care of herself. As for, Arthur, you really ought to stop him before he leaves; I think he was quite nearly finished packing when I left."

"Oh, goodness!" She sprang up and darted to the sitting room to spill some translation of the news to her mother and called for the maid to fetch her hat. As soon as it was brought, she and Rupert made their way together, rushing towards Arthur's house.

Epilogue

O n their way to the Rosewood's home, Willow could not help but think of how foolish she had been, taking someone else's word over that of Arthur himself. Had he not already reassured her of his affections? And perhaps, she should have also listened to her mother's advice all this time. All of this backwards and forwards could have very well been prevented. All the same, her and Rupert rushed towards Arthur's home to try and intercept him before he took off.

They didn't travel long down the country lane that led the way to the Rosewood estate that they spotted a figure rushing in their direction.

"That ought to be Arty himself," Rupert turned towards Willow. "Looks like he was coming to see you too."

"So it seems," Willow was a little out of breath from all the rushing.

Sure enough, it was Arthur coming towards them. His shirt was opened at the neck without a cravat around it. He looked dishevelled, which was unlike him. Willow thought he must have gotten half dressed in his travel clothes then changed his mind.

As he neared, she turned to Rupert, gave him a knowing smile, and made her way towards Arthur's direction.

The two met halfway and stopped standing in front of each other, face to face. Willow looked into Arthur's brown eyes and noticed how dilated his pupils were, how flushed his cheeks had become, and how limp his usually well maintained curls were. Yet, despite all that, she could tell he was deeply hurt.

She didn't speak to him. She knew she owed him no explanation, so she waited.

Arthur opened his mouth as if to speak, but shut it again at length.

Willow wondered if he knew that there was one way that he could make it up to her. She wondered if he would figure it out.

Rupert stood several metres away, keeping his quiet, trying not to move lest he should disturb the couple. It made no sense to him, but he knew Willow had her own way of doing things.

They stood in that way for several moments longer, Arthur bowing his head and fidgeting with his clothes. Until, he started all at once and collected WIllow into his arms.

It was a pure hug. He made no intention of kissing her, but he tried, in the only way he knew how, to let her know how he was feeling.

Willow felt a warm feeling inside of her now that he had embraced her. It was exactly what she had wanted him to do. She could feel the earnestness of his emotion. They would figure this out together.

Several months had gone by and life had almost returned to normal for WIllow, except with a few changes. Willow, Arthur and Rupert had kept their quiet about Lady Adeline's past, except to Charles. Willow felt that he ought to know from her because they had been friends for so long. Charles, at first, insisted that their engagement would not be impacted by this news at all. Willow had her thoughts, but she kept them to herself. Their engagement lasted for a few weeks, until talk of Lady Adeline having another beau in Town made its way back to Charles. So, in the end, that affair resolved itself. Amusingly, that now meant that Kitty was setting her sights on Charles once again, especially now with Arthur being taken.

Willow and Arthur were properly engaged now and a wedding was to be expected the next spring. Their families got along rather well, as Willow had hoped. Everything was quite conventional, Willow thought over to herself often, which made her content.

After all the trouble she had been through, trying to figure out what was right and what was wrong, she was content that she had done things the way she had.

Milton Keynes UK
Ingram Content Group UK Ltd.
UKHW032032191024
449814UK00010B/608

9 781944 253943